About the author

Dr Vernon Nase was a legal academic. He taught the Law of Torts, Aviation Law and the Law of Outer Space in Australia and Hong Kong. He served as Director of Mooting Programs, Academic Mentor to the Moot Court Bench, Associate Dean, Head of the Department of Law, Acting Dean, Foundation Director of the Hong Kong Centre for Maritime and Transportation Law and Foundation Director of the International ADR Mooting Competition. His great professional love has been coaching mooting teams to compete in the Space Law Mooting Competition. In semi-retirement he continues to coach Hong Kong students. He has a deep love of and commitment to the people of Hong Kong.

A MOOTIFUL LIFE!

Vernon Nase

A MOOTIFUL LIFE!

Vanguard Press

VANGUARD PAPERBACK

© Copyright 2020
Vernon Nase

The right of Vernon Nase to be identified as author of
this work has been asserted by him in accordance with the
Copyright, Designs and Patents Act 1988.

All Rights Reserved

No reproduction, copy or transmission of this publication
may be made without written permission.
No paragraph of this publication may be reproduced,
copied or transmitted save with the written permission of the
publisher, or in accordance with the provisions
of the Copyright Act 1956 (as amended).

Any person who commits any unauthorised act in relation to
this publication may be liable to criminal
prosecution and civil claims for damages.

A CIP catalogue record for this title is
available from the British Library.

ISBN 978 1 78659 39 4

*Vanguard Press is an imprint of
Pegasus Elliot MacKenzie Publishers Ltd.*
www.pegasuspublishers.com

First Published in 2020

**Vanguard Press
Sheraton House Castle Park
Cambridge England**

Printed & Bound in Great Britain

Dedication

Dedicated to:
Pui Lan
a gift from God

Acknowledgements

Thanks always to the student mooters from Australia and Hong Kong who have helped me to fill in the hours and days and nights of my life.

Preamble

MOOT (TRADITIONAL) — A DELIBERATE ASSEMBLY FOR THE ADMINISTRATION OF JUSTICE;
ONE HELD BY THE FREEMEN OF AN ANGLO-SAXON COMMUNITY.
MOOT (MODERN) — TO ARGUE AN APPEAL, BASED ON A HYPOTHETICAL LEGAL
SCENARIO, BEFORE JUDGES OR AN ARBITRAL PANEL.

In modern parlance, university law school students argue an appeal in a fictitious scenario with each team representing a different state in the dispute. Competitions cover most areas of law, including international trade law, international humanitarian law, alternative dispute resolution (arbitration, mediation and negotiation), public international law and even the law of outer space.

Nickie Jones is fifty-something. He is not a young man although for him, like many others who have immersed their life in their work, time has flown. Although he does not acknowledge it, even to himself, all those long workdays, working weekends and night lectures have taken their toll on his life. He lives for his students.

This is untypical.

In academia, where scholars trip over each other and push past each other in an effort to clamber to the top of the tree, his personal values of sacrifice are indeed untypical. We like to think that the majority of our teachers, whether it be in primary, secondary or tertiary institutions are somewhat like Mr. Chips, someone who selflessly gives their life in their true vocation. Harsh as it seems today the reality is that something is wrong with him or her in the eyes of his or her colleagues if he or she places students' interests and the general good before his own interests.

It is a truism to observe that in academia almost every academic you meet feels that he or she is the greatest academic that ever lived. Even if their accomplishments are small, they are still infected by the virus of "academic ego". It is usually terminal, as it cripples them as human beings rendering them unable to empathise with anyone but themselves. This is because they are the summit of their own purposes.

Chapter 1
The New Dean

In southern Queensland there is a marketing slogan that everyone knows, residue of a successful attempt to market the state some years previous. It is, "One day beautiful, perfect the next." It is meant to describe the blessed climate, the Florida-like climate that gives this region very mild weather during winter, where the days blend and each day brings with it a beautiful blue sky.

On this late winter's day, the sun was shining at the sandstone university when Nickie and Will stepped out into the quadrangle to make their way to the nearest café, which fed off the quadrangle into the library area. It was the days before the remodelling of the law school that separated and incarcerated or insulated staff against students by making it impossible to enter staff areas, unless you had the card or code. Even the corridors are now closed to the public and to students. However, the days when you had to make an appointment to see a member of staff, the divisive, separate days of today were not present at that time.

It was a dazzling day, so pleasant that Nickie wondered how heaven might improve on this. Perhaps it might give back to one one's youthful good looks so that one might feel like the beautiful young people who sat at the tables and chairs surrounding himself and Will. The nostalgia of it all led him to think out loud to Will and he almost regretted his words as soon as he spoke them.

"Will, they just keep getting younger every year," he said as he sipped his coffee and surveyed the young vibrant faces taking their coffee at surrounding tables.

Will was pragmatic as always. "No," he replied, "we just keep getting older each year."

"It's all relative," responded Nickie and then changed the focus of the conversation. "Hey what is this I hear about our beloved dean, Tim Taylor. Are we losing him? I hope not."

"It's confirmed. He's going overseas to the University of Vanuatu as their vice-chancellor."

"Good step up," said Nickie, "but a long way to go. How is his wife taking it?"

"Oh Regan? Well she is a bitch, but she knows his time here is limited. The VC thinks he's a bit of a crook."

Nickie paused for a moment before he spoke. "Perhaps that is the pot calling the kettle black. The VC is not exactly known as being a pinnacle of light."

"Oh, I thought you knew about Regan."

"Well, yes," said Nickie, "I suppose so. Our paths don't cross often and I'm naïve. Mertens tells me that all the time. She hasn't been friendly. I just thought she was up herself like most of our colleagues."

"She's known for her acid tongue," said Will as if putting the record right.

Nickie thought for a moment but filled the pause eventually. "Tim is complex, but he has kept things simple and been supportive of good ideas. He is a good dean as far as I can see."

"Yeah, but we're not the vice-chancellor, are we?"

"Not last time I looked."

Will had impeccable sources. He was the one to talk to about what was going on in and around the law school. "I gather they are interviewing one of the New Zealand Law deans for the job," he said.

"So we may get a New Zealander?" queried Nickie. "Does he talk properly do you know? I don't think I could handle years and years of New Zealand mispronunciation. We Aussies do a bad enough job, but they are even worse than us. When they count from one to ten you think they are requesting sex halfway through."

"Hey, don't be so hard on our brothers and sisters from across the ditch," rebuked Will.

"I know, my attempt at humour," added Nickie apologetically.

"Actually, this guy is a South African, although he likes to make out, he is a Brit."

"Not another South Effrican," mimicked Nickie.

"Looks like it." Will paused before he added, "Yeah. He was also a priest when he was younger."

Nickie was justly worried by this description.

"Sounds complex," he added as an afterthought.

The next morning Nickie was in at work early and returning from the refectory area, walking past the fountain on the left, and stepping into the expanses of the quadrangle when he saw Tim Taylor, the then dean walking towards him wheeling his bicycle.

"Hi boss," said Nickie, "they tell me you are leaving us for better things."

'Yes, VC at the University of Vanuatu."

"Amazing appointment. Congratulations. I hope that you have a wonderful time there. It has been a joy to work under you. You will be sorely missed. You encouraged a lot of people. You were always fair and supportive. You need to know you were a great law dean."

"Thank you Nickie. I appreciate your words."

"I suppose you are not that interested, but forgive me, do you know what is happening with your replacement?" asked Nickie with unnatural timidity.

"Interviews, I gather. Don't know more than that."

"Oh well, time will tell I suppose. A hard act to follow."

Chapter 2
The Interview

The interview panel was composed of the usual suspects: the vice-chancellor (it was a dean-level appointment so it fell within her brief), the Director of Research (given research profiles and rankings enjoy God-like status in most modern universities), the Director of Teaching and Learning (no doubt full of rubrics) and the obligatory Human Resources (aka personnel) person.

James Dean was somewhat ample in his physique. He looked like he had eaten one too many pork pies in his time, and consumed his lifetime's apportionment of calories already. He had a slightly swollen and rounded face, and a balding scalp. He waited for the obligatory joke about his sharing a name with the late, great actor James Dean. Of course, he did not sully his life with trivialities like a penchant for the films of the nineteen-fifties or -sixties. That was ancient history for him and culture of a sort that he could not fathom. He had neither heard of nor seen *Rebel Without a Cause* or *Giant* and he could simply see no relevance of this long-dead actor to his own life. However, he had resolved to humour the panel if they raised issues about names. And he didn't want the nickname Jimmy Dean to follow him from New Zealand to Australia.

The Vice-Chancellor, Jane Champion, seemed a somewhat weak character to James. 'Insipid' was the word that came into his mind. It warred briefly with the word 'weak', and then other words like 'feminist' and 'politically correct', unpalatable words to him, came into his mind as she spoke.

"Thank you for coming in today. We have a few basic questions for you, and then perhaps you could join us for lunch. Our Director of Research, John Thorn, will start the ball rolling."

"First what are your own research interests and where are they going? Second, how do you assess the school's research output and, third, what do you propose to do to address any perceived inadequacies?"

"As you are aware," said James, "my focus is in areas like director's liability, restitutory claims and, in particular, the law of unjust enrichment. My book on company and securities law is indisputably the seminal text in this area. It was, of course, published by Cambridge University Press."

That should appeal to the cultural cringe, thought James.

And so the interview proceeded. James felt confident that he was making his mark. It was simply not possible, in his view, for a better candidate to present.

"How would you," asked the VC, "describe your leadership style?"

"Well, I have an active style of leadership. I would not be a passive Dean of Law, just sitting back. I would get out there and interview and review the staff's teaching, scholarship and productivity and provoke improvement. We may need to prune the bush a little, but I am the man to do that. We could then bring in some exceptional scholars and that would really raise the bar on the performance of the law school. Certainly, we need to leave behind the unproductive members of staff and move into a much more dynamic and commercially relevant future."

James had the strong feeling that he was their man, that he had said exactly the right thing at the right time, and was pressing the exact right buttons. He was not a man known for his self-doubt, more perhaps for his self-righteousness.

James, from his own experiences, had a certain level of contempt that he always reserved for Human Resources Management (HRM) staff.

"Have you ever been aware of having not done as well as you would like?" said Natalie Bickerstaff, the Director of HRM at the university. "Can you give us an example and has there ever been a situation of conflict that you would like to have handled better or differently?"

James thought this a wonderful opportunity to present a martyred face to the selection panel, but of course, in the best possible way. His mind thought of the movie Lawrence of Arabia, but he did not know why, some vague memory of no particular import. Movies were not his thing.

"Well, thank you for the question, Natalie. I suppose, if I am anything, I am a martyr to my people. I work so hard I do not give myself enough rest, and I do not give my beautiful wife enough time. It is not easy for the wives of academics. I try to provide my wife with quality time, but we do have a demanding vocation. Sometimes I have be told to go home. It is a dedicated life and I like to give it everything I have."

James was eminently satisfied with his answer, but he saw the troubled look on the face of the HR lady. She rejoined.

"Thank you for your response but I was thinking of a situation of conflict. Is there anything you realised you could have done better?"

"I think I have answered that question. I tend to serve others before I serve myself." He was intent on sticking to his line rather than waking up some sleeping ghosts that might demonstrate his impatience, his petulance and his misjudgement. *Let sleeping dogs lie*, he thought.

As an afterthought James added, "I manage my staff to avoid significant conflict."

Despite an uneasiness about his answer to the final question ('Was he really who he was making himself out to be?'), the VC felt happy with the interview. She saw him as strong, but not too strong. She hoped he would be reasonably compliant and that he was a new brush, a new broom to sweep through this delinquent department who could, when they wanted to, be far too bloody-minded and resistant.

Shortly after, James was back across the ditch in New Zealand where he felt restless and anxious. This new appointment would solve his immediate little problem about his surreptitious attempt to make his book seem better than it was. If he obtained the position, he could then leave such issues behind and have a brand-new start as dean of a top-tier sandstone university. What bliss awaited him if only he were to receive that call! Still, there was always the professorship in Singapore. That might still be his, he thought, his plan B. There at least was a British influence, although dipped in a Chinese sauce. His musings were interrupted. The telephone rang and he looked briefly at the receiver before he lifted it and deigned to answer.

Chapter 3
The Announcement

Professor Noah Mertens felt betrayed by his fellow staff. He had set himself to become dean. He was the best candidate, the highest achiever, the most brilliant mind. Why was he not to be dean? Why did the staff vote en masse against his elevation into his rightful role, the role he had earned and deserved? Why? Why? Why? He could not believe there was such treachery in the ranks.

On this day Noah had the job he hated most, namely, the making of a certain announcement. He had been serving as acting dean and he faced a staff meeting full of the scum that had betrayed him. He decided to lower the announcement of the new dean on his list of items to cover at the meeting.

"I have to announce that our Vis team in Vienna was once again a spectacular performer. They made the finals and were narrowly beaten, but they had the best claimant memoranda, and David Golighty was named as the best oralist. Once again, a triumph for our mooting teams in the premier event, the Vis West."

Many of the staff had come for the new dean announcement but they still applauded vigorously. It was a success for their law school. Why should we not applaud and at least we do not have Noah as the new dean, was their thinking. It was such a relief for many there who saw him as an egotistical cad, who managed to soak up much of the law school's floating funds. Nickie made a somewhat reserved attempt to applaud for he thought Noah was overstating and overselling the performance of the team. Nickie knew full well that the team had made the knockout stages, but not the actual final, and that they had won merely Honourable Mentions for their Claimant memoranda and for one of the oralists.

"Yes, when it comes to mooting," concluded Noah, "we are simply the best."

Noah resolved to make the announcement as short and sweet. "As we all know there have been interviews for the deanship and an appointment has been made. The new dean will be Professor James Dean from Christchurch University."

Nickie found himself one of several to be chosen to buy Noah a coffee. Noah never paid. He was first into the coffee shop and he opened the door for his chosen companions before announcing that he would find a table and that he wanted a latte coffee.

Nickie found himself paying for everyone's coffee.

"He (meaning James Dean) is not an international lawyer," said Mertens. "I do not think he has ever heard of international trade law or European law. He is a philistine when it comes to mooting. This is a disastrous appointment." He paused to allow those present to soak up what he saw as the inadequacies of the new Dean.

"You see how well we did in the Vis Moot again. Wasn't this outstanding?"

There was no option among the onlookers at the table but to nod and mumble their agreement obediently as Noah was not known to take dissent kindly. "I understand that he wants to be considered to be an Englishman, but, of course, you know he is from South Africa. Furthermore, he has a reputation for being difficult and he cannot think beyond his own interests, restitution huh! I think he should be restored to Africa. He will not be a success. Well, the staff have what they want. They will get what they deserve. It is their loss."

As he looked around the table at his coffee partners, he repeated himself once again as if to underline his own comparative brilliance. "He will not last."

Chapter 4
The Retreat

As the bus neared the retreat site, which was somewhere on the Darling Downs of Queensland, in rural Queensland, many kilometres away from any diversion, the atmosphere was gloomy. A sense of unease was felt by most on board. Why were they being dragged all this way if not for some kind of Stalinist or Maoist re-education event?

"Stalag 17?" quipped Nickie.

"I know nothing," responded Will with tongue in cheek.

"If this is *Hogan's Heroes*, who is Captain Klink?"

"Who do you think?"

A burning bush?

The new dean, James Dean, walked backwards and forwards across the stage, as he delivered his address to the staff. It seemed to Nickie that he was attending a church service.

"When the centre is experiencing funding cuts, there is an undeniable need to make cuts. Think of it this way, if you are a farmer you will have to cut back the bushes so that they can grow to full vigour. It is only when you prune the bush that the tree can grow with increased vigour to deliver a bumper harvest. We must clear away the dead wood to grow our tree. We have no choice if we are to become successful."

Nickie found himself thinking of the old Hollywood era and Cecil B. DeMille's movie *The Ten Commandments*, starring Charlton Heston as Moses. He rejected his thoughts but then James said, "I am a shepherd and you are my flock," and Nickie felt the analogy of the burning bush was somehow sound. James seemed at that moment more like a charismatic preacher than a law dean.

Almost involuntarily Nickie thought, *So this is how he is going to lead us out of the desert, by sacking people and employing those who supported his vision of the law as a narrow, insular, contract-driven entity.* Nickie knew his view on the new dean was pejorative and he knew he would have to bite his tongue, in a manner of speaking, or else his tenure would cease to exist. Part of him did not want to stay within an educational institution driven by such a limited vision. He soon was to feel even more unhappy.

Nickie lifted the telephone handset and found it was Will.

"Have you seen Jimmy Dean yet? He's walking the corridors to see who is in. I think he writes it down."

"Okay, I'll leave the door ajar. Anyway, I am always in, always here beavering away."

"Oh, I'm sorry Nickie. I didn't realise you were a crawler."

"No, just have a long way to drive so always get in early and stay late."

'You should live in Brisbane," said Will. "You don't even like the sun, so why live on the coast?"

Some things just evolve thought Nickie, but he was silent.

The crows were amazingly loud at the sandstone university. They hung around the trees at the edges of the quadrangle, and hapless lecturers at times were almost drowned out by the noise they made. The pathos of the university was added to at night by the plaintive cries of the curlews, who lived in stands of bamboo on this most beautiful of all campuses. The main quadrangle café, on the other hand, suffered at the hands of the ibis. On this day several were making a nuisance of themselves by jumping onto tabletops, upsetting the plates and cutlery, and causing glasses and cups to overturn. Inevitably there were crashes and the staff rushed out to shoo the clumsy predators away. Nickie placed the coffee cups on the table, one at his own spot and the other in front of Will.

"I have news," said Will as he sipped his coffee. "I think we may lose our mooting guru, Professor Mertens."

"Why is that?"

"Well, Dean has started on his interviews of staff. He seems to have started the purging. Evidently he told Noah that he wanted to shut down mooting."

"Wow, really! That extreme. How did Mertens take it? Not well I imagine."

"He took immediate leave. The rumour mill says he won't be back."

Nickie pondered things for a long moment in time and space. Then he replied.

"Wow, that *is* a big scalp."

"And I think he is starting to recruit. That may not be good for us, as neither of us really have protectors, someone who will speak up for us and who he may listen to. I believe I am on his hit list. That is what my source tells me. I do not think you are necessarily on it but there is something else that might not leave you happy."

"You may not want to hear it and I do not want to say anything to make your life harder than it already is."

"You had better tell me. Your source has a one hundred percent hit rate so, even if it leaves me swearing out loud, please tell me."

"Sorry mate but I've heard that they are interviewing a UK academic whose specialty area is the law of torts."

"And restitution?" chimed in Nickie.

"Yes."

"So all those teaching excellence nominations mean nothing."

"Brave new world here."

Dean James Dean had indeed set about interviewing staff, sitting in on lectures, purging some old staff, and hiring new staff. He was active. In Nickie's case, he chose to sit in on an evening lecture given by Nickie. It was a Doctor of Jurisprudence (JD) group, composed mostly of professionals who were garnering a law degree to add to their medical, science or engineering degrees. They lacked the innocence of an early year undergraduate bachelor of laws group. And they were not easily intimidated by age or status.

Nickie was in summary mode. "So, to review, so far we have seen that economic loss by way of a latent defect in a structure may lead to liability. We have seen how the law conceptualises this loss as economic loss in cases like Caltex and the Willemstad, Murphy and Brentwood Shire Council and Bryan and Maloney. Chief Justice De Jersey also explained the rationalisation in the Todd Group case. We have seen also the categories of subsequent purchasers as potential plaintiffs with possible defendants being the original builder, the architect, the engineer or perhaps, arguably, the local authority. Hard now to succeed against the local authority, but there are some cases on the books where actions have succeeded. The exception rather than the rule.

"We have also seen the High Court's overly conservative approach to this type of loss in Woolcock Street Investments."

Nicky could see James Dean squirming as he struggled to contain his opinions. Feeling he had nothing to lose, and hoping his students would rise to the challenge of James' views about the obsolescence of tort law, he decided to be inclusive.

"James you seem a little restless. Is there something you would like to add? Please feel free."

The dam had been breached and James waded into the water.

"Yes. I really do not see the point of any kind of liability persisting under tort law. This is far better to be dealt with exclusively under contract law."

The students en masse turned to look towards the back of the lecture room where James had been sitting.

"Yes," said Gary. "But what about the contracts they force onto inexperienced purchasers? They use standard terms that they will refuse to alter. The purchasers have no choice but to sign."

"Well," responded James, being someone who rarely backed away from an argument or filed his want to always be right, "they could have self-protected. There is a principle in contract law of the buyer beware and must face the legal consequences of failing to self-protect."

"I was a builder," said Gary, "and I tell you that defects can be disguised, and materials can be substituted. Pipes, for example, are easy to lay, have the inspection and be replaced with a smaller gauge."

"Yes," added Mary, "what about subsequent purchasers?"

James was never devoid of a reply. "They can get the seller to warrant the property. As I said, 'buyer beware'. They can conduct inspections."

"We should not lose sight," said Brett, "of the fact that we are dealing with latent defects that are invisible in nature until, down the line, they manifest and necessitate expensive repairs. From an engineer's perspective, and that is what I do for a living, you have to rely on the original engineer's calculations. Otherwise, it would be necessary to deconstruct a building, to find out what you really need to do to address the issue or if there is an issue. And, of course, it is simply not feasible to destroy buildings to ascertain the true nature of the sub-soil."

Nickie decided it was time to take control back. He didn't know if it was too soon, but he did not want things to descend to positional statements about the relative worth and roles of contract law as against the law of negligence. *Better to assume control sooner than later,* he thought. He went into tennis umpire mode. There was a certain 'Thank you ball boys' tone to his words.

"Thank you, James. Thank you, students. That was a really valuable exchange of views. I would like to bring us back to the case of Woolcock Street Investments, in which the plaintiff subsequent purchaser did not succeed. Justice Kirby in dissent did observe that "[i]t may not be alleged that there is a breach of contract to the first purchaser, but there is alleged to be a breach of proper standards of care in the performance of your professional duties. Kirby has raised the possibility of a professional negligence action. Do you think he is right to do so? He was in dissent."

Nickie met Will for coffee, a regular ritual for them both.

"Well," said Will, "I have to start looking for a new job, a new university in which to teach, or to go back into practice in some way."

"You're gone?" queried Nickie with a deep sense of dread growing within him.

"Yes."

"What did he say to you?"

"No new contract for me."

"Why? Did he offer a reason?"

"He waffled on about number of articles published and how planning law was not a priority and that he had others who could teach criminal law."

"You did complete your PhD and you do have an adequacy of scholarly articles."

"Not enough for him. O'Hara is trying to buy his way back in by offering to write joint articles with him. It might work but I could never do that, especially with such a jerk."

Will paused and looked at Nickie with a 'you too' expression on his face. "I see your replacement arrived last week, fresh from the UK. Has he asked you to come in for an interview?"

"No. He emailed me after sitting in to congratulate me on my teaching. And I have a continuing appointment."

"You know they are offering redundancies?"

"Yes, I am tempted," said Nickie. My vistas are not exactly endless, since they appointed the UK guy. You know, he gave a presentation to the staff and waffled on about Occam's razor. I think he has the wrong line on economic loss, but they swallowed everything he said hook, line and sinker. Of course, the executive dean of business and law is just an accountant. He wouldn't understand."

"Have you met the new lecturer from China?" asked Will.

"Yes. His name is Zhao Wei. He just kind of grunted at me when I tried to say hello. He's from one of the western provinces of China so maybe good scholarship but not so great with English. Probably a good idea to recruit someone to teach about the Chinese legal system and also about their version of trade law."

"Yes, except Dean has announced that he will teach contract law."

"What experience does someone from the west of China, a civil law country, have with a common-law-based contract law?" said Nickie while shrugging his shoulders, then they turned back to contemplate their respective futures.

Soon Professor Zhao Wei stood before the class of several hundred students, as he gave his first lecture in contract law. He was part of the way through and felt very isolated. The task of learning common law contract law with little time for preparation was challenging in the extreme.

"Advertisement is offer to treat. We call invitation to treat. I sell you food from my catalogue it is invitation to treat. You make offer when you buy food."

He had heard that in western law schools they teach Socratic style. While this is not a practice uniformly followed in Australian law schools, Zhao felt the need to at minimum throw out questions.

"What is difference between offer and invitation to treat?"

There is always one person in every group who can be tempted to test the boundaries between respect and testing a lecturer. A single hand rose above the throng.

"Yes," said Zhao.

"There is no difference," opined Jack Spratt with his tongue firmly planted in his cheek.

"No," retorted Zhao with stern visage. "You must read case, Carlill (horribly mispronounced by Zhao) Carbolic Smoke Ball Company.

"You must have intention," stated Zhao.

For a brief moment Jack, one of the less sympathetic students among his cohort, dwelt on the thought of asking Zhao what the word "treat" means as it is a relatively uncommon word and Zhao's standard of English was in question in Spratt's mind.

"Offer more than invitation," stated Zhao.

What is difference between invitation to treat and offer to world?"

A gloomy silence descended upon the lecture theatre. Eyes looked down upon iPads and other devices and minds redirected to social media and away from anything like eye contact.

It was such a painful silence. Zhao felt angry now at the lack of responsiveness. The respect he always felt in Qinghai was missing in action here. Why were they not responding?

Chapter 5
A New Hope?

As a direct result of an avalanche of complaints about Zhao, a meeting of the law school inner circle was called. It was not a formal meeting, but it was called to discuss the contract law class. It was a very directed meeting with the dean, the newly appointed Deputy Dean, Ron Graham from New Zealand and Greg Bentley, an associate professor who had been around in that law school for a very long time. Greg looked after teaching allocations.

Ron Graham opened up discussions. "The students are up in arms about Professor Zhao. They claim they cannot understand him. It's a language thing. His spoken English is sub-standard at this stage. I wondered whether or not we should pull him from the class and give him a bit more time to settle in."

"And to perfect his English," added James. "The worst thing we can do is to leave him there. His scholarship speaks for itself and it will be valuable, and his teaching too, when it comes to elective subjects." He paused for a moment's reflection. "Can we explore some options? Is there anyone who we can substitute in this subject?"

"No, not at this stage," said Greg. "Literally everyone is already overloaded. If they didn't feel the need to impress our new dean, they would be arriving in waves complaining about their excessive teaching as the allocations currently stand."

The deputy dean added his perception to the conversation. "And the budget is tight to say the least."

"I'll teach it myself if I have to," announced James. And then dismissively, he added, "I've done it before, and it is only short term. We can get tutors to mark the assignments and exams. I simply do not want any complaints to the executive dean or PVC (pro- vice chancellor) at this early stage of my tenure. I have to attend a meeting in the Chancery so I will leave you now to discuss this. If all else fails I will teach the subject."

The meeting in the Chancery was important to maintain the law school's international exchange programmes and profile. Of course, James Dean was not an internationalist. He believed in commercial law, but not so much in international law, which he saw as an affectation, and international trade law he saw as a body of law that was misguided in seeking to find international conventions and universally accepted rules to guide business. He thought that a micro-approach was better, one that was based on contract law rather than rules developed by European scholars. The Vice Chancellor, Jane Champion, attended along with the Pro-Vice-chancellor (Research), John Thorn, James Dean and two distinguished visitors. They were

Professor Li from the Chinese University of Beijing, and Professor Schneider from Berlin University. Both universities were joined in exchange programmes with the law school. The university supported the forging of such links, especially with the Asian powerhouse country, China. They wanted to be able to point to international collaboration. Their agenda was to broaden such collaborations, and to forge greater research linkages. The immediate agenda was to transact a continuation of the existing arrangements.

Both the vice-chancellor and the pro-vice-chancellor spoke about the existing arrangements and their desire to consolidate and broaden such arrangements. They wanted more, and they wanted to see what suggestions might arise from the brains trust assembled at that venue on that day. All was auspicious as the team worked over the existing arrangements, except that James was quiet and chose the path of joining in, rather than seeking to lead or participate.

Professor Li spoke last. In concluding, he observed, "The past is only the beginning. There are many areas in which we can collaborate." This was an auspicious conclusion, one they could build upon.

A great shock followed. "Well, yes," said James Dean, "but one of those is not human rights. People don't have human rights in China, do they? You repress freedom of speech, and you eradicate those who propose it. And your legal system is not about doing justice. It just perpetuates the dominance of the clique who control the party. Your system is pure cronyism. What do we really have to learn from you?"

Professor Li was speechless. Not so Professor Schneider who rejoined, "I think that you are being a little unfair. If we do not collaborate, we never become friends, and we certainly do not generate change."

"I do not think that you can talk," spat out James, "Adolf did not exactly promote freedom. He was a fascist and human rights were not particularly high on his agenda if you were Jewish or if you opposed him."

"That was then, this is now," spat out Schneider. "Anyway, your country was not so kind to its indigenous population in the past. You put them in chains." He paused before stating, "I think this meeting has come to an end."

Li added, "You are not Chinese. You should not judge Chinese. I go too."

"But gentlemen, what about lunch?" pleaded Professor Thorn.

Schneider was decisive and icy in reply. "There will be no lunch."

They left a room bathed in stony silence.

"I think the meeting is over too," said James as he rose to leave.

"We need to talk about this," prompted the vice-chancellor.

"Sorry, I have a contract law class to teach." For once, James was pleased to have an unassailable excuse.

"You'll have to make an appointment," he said superciliously. He quickly left the room.

The vice-chancellor allowed only flickers of emotion to cross her face. Thorn, on the other hand, was less controlled. "What is wrong with this man?" he exclaimed passionately. "He has to be a fruitcake!"

The corridor speaks.

Nickie worked long hours. Some of his teaching was at night, and he liked to work until he had everything truly wrapped up each day. As early as between six p.m. and seven p.m. on certain nights the corridors were relatively empty. The Deputy Dean, Professor Ron Graham, had an office off the corridor, not far from Nickie's pokey room. The rooms off the corridor were not particularly soundproof.

On this night, when Nickie walked down the corridor in the direction of the rest room, everything was relatively still and quiet. You could hear a pin drop and with those sandstone walls and elevated ceiling, there was a natural kind of amplification. Nickie could hear certain noises coming from within Ron's office. "Uh, uh, uh." The noises were unmistakably those of two adult persons engaged in sexual intercourse. When Nickie returned from the rest room, walking towards his office parallel to Graham's office, the moaning was still going on.

He doesn't say much but at least one part of his body is working, thought Nickie.

Chapter 6
Suicide

Dean James Dean stood before a large lecture theatre full of students. The students seemed a bit restless, with some listening and some sneaking looks at social media on their laptops. A torpid atmosphere prevailed in that lecture theatre, as if the cobwebs that were being formed on the ceiling carried a greater level of interest than the words of the learned professor in front of them.

Dean James Dean continued his lecture.

"There should not ever be the need to imply terms into contracts. The terms should always be express and then it all boils down to the interpretation of what is expressly included in the contract. However unwisely, it is not to ensure all terms are expressed, there are some situations where the law unwisely implies terms, supposedly on the basis of ensuring business efficacy. This can occur where it is 'reasonable and equitable' to do so. They must be necessary to give business efficacy... er..."

James Dean paused, because he could sense the feeling of apathy coming from his students, and he was vaguely aware that their attention was more likely to be focused on social media, than on his own significant and learned opinions and the learning content of the lecture. He could feel the students' restless spirits and it angered him. He felt his fists tighten and he took a long, hard slow look at the disinterested rabble that he felt comprised his audience.

Then he began his rant.

"All you young people think about is sex. I'll have you know that my wife and I lead an active sex life."

The students looked up in surprise. He had at last secured their attention. But now he wanted both to vindicate himself and to give his students a lesson.

As James uttered the fateful words, "For example…," all around the lecture theatre personal recorders turn on. The evidence gathering had commenced.

That afternoon, following a deputation of law students, the Executive Dean of Law and Business, Ron Roots, requested an urgent meeting with the vice-chancellor. There was a suicide rapidly followed by an execution, when he handed the VC a copy of the audiotape submitted by the students. But, of course, all this occurred behind closed doors.

Chapter 7
Noah the Mooting Guru

Professor Noah Mertens enjoyed being free of his wife for this particular trip away with his mooting team. The trips away with his mooting teams were grand in scale, as they involved the team honing its skills in a number of pre-moot competitions in various European countries.

Although the travels involved long hours and long sessions with his mooting team, they still afforded him opportunity, when his wife did not accompany him, to avail himself of certain services offered in the 'red light districts' of the cities he knew well.

He also had a tendency to select at least some members of his teams, the female members, not just for their intelligence and their research or oral advocacy skills, but also for the possibility of somehow seducing one or two along the way. This was one of those trips where he was able to achieve this goal.

The sex as far as he was concerned was always good and he liked to live on the edge, the edge of being discovered, the edge of disgrace. It was part of the thrill of the chase and, when all was said and done, he was confident of controlling the emotions of the young women who fell for him. He liked his conquests as much for the control and dominance he achieved in those transitory relationships, as for the sex. It was always about him. He was in his own words and in his own mind, 'simply the best'. In any event he had the assurance of being a devout Catholic. Being a devout Catholic was for him a license to sin because his sins were always forgiven, no matter how many times he repeated the same sins. He lived in an unlimited pool of forgiveness for himself certainly, not always for those who dissented or crossed him. That was his way.

When his mooter, Maria, rolled over to look at his face after the sex, he simply stated what he wanted and, because he was so brilliant, this simply had to be the case.

"Maria, having sex with me should inspire you to speak well, to moot well, and to win tomorrow's competition. You will moot the best you have ever mooted and win, yes?"

Maria wasn't sure quite how to react, but she knew he was a man of firm opinions and to humour him.

"Of course. But just one more practice."

Maria was tired the next day and emotionally in her own place, apart from others. Her mooting was competent, but not great. The team did not win through to the final.

Back in Australia at the sandstone university after all the excitement of travel and competition, Professor Noah Mertens now stood before the assembled staff as acting dean, pending the taking up by the new dean of his position.

"Now I have to report the good news on the Vis team. They were a great success. They made the final. They won the Best Oralist Award and they also won Best Memorandum Award. This was a truly great performance."

When Will and Nickie sat down for coffee, Nicky observed that the Vis team had done very well.

"Noah has a tendency to exaggerate his successes," observed Will. "He was very optimistic about their performance. They made the semi-finals not the final and their awards were Highly Commended Awards, Highly Commended Oralist and Memoranda, not the Best Oralist or the Best Memoranda. He exaggerates results so frequently that people disbelieve it when he actually wins a moot. They think he is just exaggerating again."

"The girl who cried 'fire'," mused Nickie.

"Yes, the professor who cried best, best, I am the best and nothing but the best …"

"When only the best will do," rejoined Nickie. They laughed.

"Something like that."

Mertens was chastened by the summons to meet with the dean, James Dean. His usual bravado was missing. He felt bleak, in a hopeless position after the staffs' great betrayal by not getting behind him for the deanship position. He knew the new dean, the infidel

James Dean, would be enjoying a honeymoon period, within which time everything he did would be endorsed, blessed and supported wholly by the university establishment. He found his troubled mind still going over things when he sat on the other side of the table to Dean Dean. His innate stubbornness told him not to give off much emotion, to not let the dean see that he was getting to him, no matter how outrageous the proposition was that was being presented by the dean. His instinct for survival was strong. His ego was great. His desire to ultimately exceed and undermine was still present. His critical faculties were ripped and ready to go. He thought the best approach was for his reactions, to whatever bitter pill the dean was forcing him to swallow, needed to be restrained and that he needed to feign a certain emotional distance.

"I plan," announced James once the pleasantries were over, "to close down the mooting programme of the school. In my view money could be much better spent than in encouraging an elitist activity such as this mooting."

Despite his promise to himself to play his cards close to his chest and to not react, Noah could not restrain himself.

"But we have an international reputation for excellence and international law in a shrinking world will remain of paramount importance."

Dean announced his grand plan with pride and bravado. "There will be no more mooting and there will be no 'Vis' team and no world tour of pre-moots. We will, instead, become a commercially oriented law school and will focus on the contract driven aspects of the law, and other more practical and industry driven areas of study. We will not obsess over international law. Our plans will include the establishment of barrister's chambers in the city, and the creation of a professional legal training course bridging that gap between law school and the legal industry. We will be commercial not international." Dean eased himself back in his chair. "That is just the way it is going to be."

Noah Mertens felt like a schoolboy who had just been reprimanded by the principal of his school. He felt chastened, although he knew himself well enough to understand that a deep vent of anger and desire for revenge was going to well up inside himself in the fullness of time.

"The university is used to us succeeding and to pointing at these successes. A law school that does not moot is hardly a law school at all. That is your choice and I shall consider my options," said Noah, half speaking to himself in answer to his inner voice.

Noah's departing function was small scale for a man whose actions were larger than life. It was conducted in the foyer of the law school in the evening during a mid-semester break. Dean was unable to attend due to travel overseas. Thus, his deputy, Professor Ron Graham, filled in for him. Graham was not noted for his communication skills generally, especially his speech-making. Indeed, Nickie and Will mused together about how he managed to teach at all. Generally speaking, he was a man of few words. Nickie portrayed him as being 'the man without a personality'. Will was harsher in his words although attempting to communicate something similar. 'The man who can't communicate' seemed harsher to Nickie, who wanted to give him the benefit of the doubt, for he knew he must have something working for him to attract the women, despite seeming to possess a very flat, humourless personality.

"I want to thank Professor Mertens for his contribution to the law school, both as a scholar and as a mooting coach. We are sad to lose you to the Perth University, but know that it will give to you the opportunities that you seek. This is a small token of our appreciation for your many years of work within the law school." He handed across an elaborately wrapped present.

"It's a bottle of castor oil," whispered Will in Nickie's ear.

Chair Professor Noah Mertens replied. "I am," he said, "very proud of what I have achieved in our mooting programme. I have aimed for excellence and, as I say to my mooters, excellence is open ended. You will see. I will create more excellence in the West where I will be dean of the law school, where we will embrace international excellence, a place where 'international' will be a good word, not a bad word."

There were great symmetries between the speeches that Noah made. More than once over the years was it suggested that he basically only ever wrote or made the one speech, he simply kept re-jigging the same speech to fit the cloth that he wore on any given day.

"He offered you a job?" asked Will incredulously. He could not believe Nickie's news.

"Yes. And I accepted it. Let's face it, there is nothing left for me here. They have employed a tort teacher at a higher level than myself, so my franchise is in process of being withdrawn. Whether I like it or not, my time here is limited. I would rather be proactive than relegated. I know Mertens is not easy."

"Some might see him as a right bastard," said Will. "Unlike me you can see his positives."

With very little fuss, Nickie left the sandstone university. He and his wife, Bianca, drove from the east coast across the country all the way to Western Australia. They managed to avoid stray kangaroos, a mob of emus and the occasional snake that shimmied across the highway. They stood on the lookout over the great Australian Bight and the Great Southern Ocean. Contrary to expectation it rained as they crossed the Nullarbor Plains en route to Perth, the most isolated capital city in the world. It was a great adventure, but they stood on the crest of an unknown world and an unrevealed life in 'the west' as Australians would call it. When they arrived, they stayed at on campus accommodation for a week. At dusk small rabbits would appear. They saw no snakes but there were lots of warning signs about the 'wrigglies', the poisonous dugites that were there, but just out of sight.

Professor Noah Mertens moved seamlessly from the east coast of Australia to the west coast of the same continent thanks to his first-class tickets. The lecture theatre was full of bright-eyed first year students. That first day of newness, sometimes of idealism, the joy of achievement, the possibilities that every soul felt would ripen into a worthwhile, and for some, lucrative career. There was a bubble there that needed a dose of reality, but not one to be quashed. Noah chose on this day not to provide the wise counsel the students deserved, and needed to help them deal with the mesmerising reality of law school. It was a place that should inspire, but where instead, all too frequently, an individual's dreams and ideals could be driven into the dust by selfish, non-caring academic staff. Conversely, it was also often a place where caring staff were met by a tsunami of student expectations of success unmatched by any dedication or commitment, an unpreparedness on their part to do the hard yards needed to master the challenging discipline that was the law. And the ever-present Law Student Association stood in the background so ready to corrupt all idealism, helping students to learn how to take shortcuts and to lose themselves (and sometimes their self-esteem) in a booze-soaked life of binge drinking and indulgence. And at the new university, there were also those who so devalued the amount of work required by a traditional degree like the Bachelor of Laws so profoundly, that they worked full time while also enrolling in full time studies. The real world is composed of such diversity, but this did not worry Professor Noah Mertens as he surveyed the assembled first year cohort. "Yes," he concluded, "we will aim for excellence; we seek the best when only the best will do. This is because we are simply the best." The students gave to the sage dean the respect that was due and applauded his speech. Noah returned to his seat with a look of triumph on his face as his internal voice noted his own brilliance. How could they not be impressed by him?

The coffee shop was nicely put together with lots of wood panelling and wooden surfaces and tasteful carpet. It stood in stark contrast to the Besser block and basic exteriors found in most places at the university, apart from the chancery which was red brick also with quality interiors. The administration of the university and the vice-chancellor inhabited the pertinently named Chancery.

Mertens had invited Nickie to have coffee, but when they entered, he said that he would find a table and that he wanted a latte coffee.

"So," he said, "you will establish a Moot Court Bench and coach your specialty moot and mentor the other coaches. I will, of course, coach a team in the Vis West Moot as I have done for so many years at that other place." Mertens had become accustomed to referring to the sandstone university as 'that other place'. It was not directly derisory, but it conveyed his studied indifference.

The Moot Court Bench was an American institution, where a discrete group of students would engage in mentoring and encouraging mooting activities within the law school. They would run seminars to train first year students, stage junior and senior mooting competitions, training sessions and stage special events with practitioners giving speeches or lectures on advocacy in its many forms. Mertens had established a Moot Court Bench at the sandstone university and he was about to import the concept to the West with Nickie as its foundation mentor.

"What is the student culture like here?" asked Nickie feeling a little like he had ridden into the valley of the ten thousand. He was leading the charge, while Mertens could safely sit on a hilltop surveying the battlefield and claim all credit if things went well. He thought, *Perhaps Mertens' capacity to exaggerate to claim credit is indeed legendary* and, for a split second, he wondered what he had done to himself.

"You know. They do not really know what quality mooting is like, but you can teach them. It will be easy for you. And when you get the Moot Court Bench up and going, they will make it a lot easier for everyone. It is a piece of cake. By the way you did not get *me* any cake to go with the coffee. This is not very good."

Nickie scurried to the counter and dutifully returned with cake and more questions to ask.

"Don't worry about the Law Students Association," assured Mertens. I have reached an agreement, where we will create a special fund under their control and out of the reach of the central administration. There will be enough money to fund them and, more importantly, to fund international mooting for the next three years. And the university will not have control of the funds. They will be student funds. It is so brilliant. I have outsmarted the financial boffins once again. I ask the students to send over money, and they give it to me every time we send a mooting team away."

"So what other moots do you anticipate that we will do? And who will coach what?" enquired Nickie.

"We must do the Jessup Moot. It is the premier international law moot in the world. Not as significant as the Willem C. Vis Moot, but everyone does it and we can make our mark, especially if we can make the top four or top two in Australia. All the group of eight universities compete, and we must compete too. We will also compete in the Maritime Law Arbitration Moot and you must coach in the Space Law Moot and I will do the Vis Moot."

"Who are you getting to coach the Jessup and Maritime Law Moots?"

"Karen Hoffmann will coach the Jessup and we have a downtown practitioner, Stewart Pisconi, who will take on the Maritime Moot team."

"Do they have any experience at coaching?" Nickie enquired.

"No. But that is not essential at this stage." Nickie knew from the tone of Noah's voice that this was a non-contestable zone. He felt that anger was lurking close to the surface, and that a sharp reaction, which ought to accompany such an immature decision, would follow if he said anything negative about the decision. It was not that Mertens, he thought, was evil or intolerant or a tyrant, but he was an alpha male, and alpha males do not like to be denied or resisted. He was already making excuses for Mertens. He also resisted this thought.

"Anyway, you can show an interest in them," said Professor Noah Mertens. "You can help them out. They will be fine."

Nickie weakened and offered an opinion as he strayed onto the minefield. "It does take a few years for coaches to grow into the role before they can get to my level, and then a few more years, quite a few more years, before they can approach your transcendent level of competence." He had tried hard to massage Mertens' ego but, ultimately, it could never have been enough. Mertens now clearly saw himself as a God professor in the European sense of the word.

"The Moot Court Bench can assist the newer coaches, and you are responsible in any event for the Moot Court."

"Of course," said Nickie, but internally he squirmed at the thought of having to guide colleagues where he was unsure that they would receive his guidance or show the necessary higher-level commitment needed to achieve success.

"Oh, by the way," added Mertens, as if he were uttering a minor afterthought, "I will be away to deliver a paper at the Cross-cultural Law Conference on a yacht in the Mediterranean. You will have to act as dean in my absence. There will be nothing for you to do. Marnie, my PA, will do most things for you. You only have to attend one meeting with the executive dean of business to review some matters. You do not have to prepare anything for that. You just sit back and listen and *don't* say anything. That is how it works. You will see. It is no work for you at all."

I suppose I will not receive an allowance for this, thought Nickie but chose to respond with a simple, factual question. "How long are you away?"

"Only about four weeks, then I have to go to London to teach an intensive there. It coincides with Wimbledon. My wife enjoys Wimbledon, and you know how devoted I am to her. I am a one-woman man. I always love my wife. She is the only one ever for me." He paused and Nickie wondered. "That will take another couple of weeks. When I return I shall choose a

Vis team. They will be the best, simply the best when only the best will do."

The Vis Team

Several months later the students selected in the Vis team, Alexander ('Alex') Watts, Fiona ('Fifi') McGrath, Daniel ('Danny') Duval, Rebecca ('Rebel') Russell, Linda Liu (Lulu) and Christine ('Chrissie') Garlett trickled into the law school boardroom, and sat at the long central table. Noah Mertens duly strode to the chair position at the head of the table.

"You are chosen," he said, "because you are the best students in this law school, the best it can offer. But that is not enough because there is another mountain to scale. It is an Everest because it requires a huge amount of work and dedication in which you will *never* say no to my invitations for you to work harder. Then you have the opportunity to become the best of the best.

"You are given a huge factual scenario in this arbitration. Whether you represent the claimant or the respondent in this arbitration, if you are asked a question," said Mertens, "how will you answer it?"

"I find the right law," responded Rebel, "to answer it, and tell them what the correct law and interpretation is."

"I would give them the facts that support my interpretation," added Danny.

"Remember this," said Mertens, "facts first then law and application and, finally, to a policy reason in favour of your interpretation. You know what I mean by policy?" There were nods, but there was also a deep doubt in the eyes of at least some of the team and Noah picked up on their doubt, their insecurity or diffidence and continued. "Policy can be a reason why it is best to decide a matter in the way they have suggested. For example, it does not then create a bad precedent, something that will affect society or business efficacy adversely in the future in like situations. Don't create a dangerous precedent or decision. The proposition is straight forward enough."

Mertens was on a roll so he decided to continue and to throw in an example from his past teams. "In order to prepare for the oral rounds of the competition, we practise moot relentlessly and we maintain a bank of questions asked, and we prepare model answers for those questions. In one of my winning teams our mooter was asked a question, a very difficult question, but he had already thought it through, and he had a model answer at his disposal. My mooter leaned back as if he didn't know the answer, and to convey that the question was very difficult. But then, as if he had a sudden insight, he suddenly gave the pre-prepared answer. It was acting on his part, pure and simple, and it had maximum impact with the judges because they thought it was a spontaneous impromptu answer. This is what we sometimes do. We maximise our marks through performance."

Mertens was not done yet. "When you make an argument, you should have at least two sub-arguments in support. You can have three things in support of each contention. First should always be facts, then law applied to the facts to support your assertion and finally, as I mentioned, you can go to policy reasons, why it makes good policy, avoids bad outcomes, promotes social unity, does not set a dangerous precedent."

"So," said Mertens, "we start next on the problem to map the issues we need to research. We will whiteboard this. You need to come ready to offer your insight into the problem. We will slice and dice the problem, which reminds me of the most important thing. For each meeting one of you is responsible for bringing in a cake. It is an essential part of the meeting. That is it. Go to work now!"

The first of many meetings concluded without coffee and cake but Mertens was soon able to feed, like an academic *'Jabba the Hutt'* on the food procured by his students. It was just a small slice of things to come.

Mertens' house was modest enough, but you just knew he had purchased it for a song and would make money when he eventually came to sell it. His wife Ava was loyal and pleasant. When Nickie and his wife arrived, he found himself wondering how long she had been suffering. His thoughts were soon answered when, over dinner, Noah unilaterally raised the issue of his marriage to Ava. "I am," he pronounced with vigour, "a one-woman man. I love my wife. She is truly the love of my life, the only woman for me."

At this point Nickie and Bianca shared a glance and Nickie thought, *Methinks he does proclaim too much. Perhaps he is the opposite of what he claims.* It was a cynicism that Nickie rarely felt, but sometimes people give themselves away when they over-compensate.

"How is your moot going at this stage?" asked Nickie.

"Excellent. One of the girls is crap as a scholar, but the rest of them are brilliant. I should be able to squeeze absolute high-quality memoranda out of them. You know they do the claimant memorandum first and then they respond in their respondent submissions to a team allocated to them. They answer and rebut that team's claimant memorandum. I am waiting eagerly for their first draft. But you know, of course, I never... *never* read the first draft. They always get it back. That is part of my coaching technique. I want nothing but the best and first drafts are always a mess, so I do not waste my time on them."

"Oh, interesting," responded Nickie who wondered how that might look and how his team would respond if he were callous enough to try that caper on them. *It is not for me*, he thought.

A day or two later the Vis Moot team members filed through the door of the law school boardroom. Mertens was clinically premeditated in keeping them waiting. He strode into the room decisively and it seemed that steam was coming out of his ears such was the anger that he exuded.

"You have submitted your first draft of the memorandum on time. That is good. But what you did with your time in preparing this I do not know!"

As Dean Mertens threw the elaborate and carefully constructed memoranda of many pages onto the table with force, he continued. "This (he paused as his face was starting to turn scarlet with anger) this thing is crap... *crap!* You are wasting my precious time! Go away! Talk about this among yourselves but go away and fix this up. It is so bad it is not even worthy of my comments! I give you forty-eight hours to fix this before I disband the team. This is pathetic."

At that Mertens stood and walked out of the room. He did not forget to take a piece of cake with him. He had made his point. Now he wanted his cake, and he wanted to eat it too.

Later in the day, when he was taking coffee with Nickie and Professor Francisco Kreuger, Mertens mimicked his own performance.

"'This is crap!' I told them! I gave them forty-eight hours to fix it. I deserved an academy award. My acting was indescribably brilliant. I even tried to hold my breath to turn red. It should have been taped. I was masterful."

Humility is definitely not one of the attributes of our glorious leader, thought Nickie. He was beginning to feel that in many situations the end justified the means for Mertens.

"I am presuming you actually read some of the memoranda," said Nickie tentatively although he instantly regretted having done so, in case scorn was kindled and directed against him.

"Of course not. Well, I did read a passage or two and it seemed quite good, but that is not the point. It has to be the best and as soon as possible. This way we win awards. We win the moot! That is what it is all about."

"This is not 'the other place'," said Nickie and he knew that he was pushing the rim of what Mertens would tolerate. "The students may struggle with the complex content."

"Yes, but I have the best students here," said Mertens. "You are right', he conceded after a pause, "it is not 'the other place', but we have to aim as high and we need to achieve more and sooner with our teams."

"Noah," said Francisco, who was always ready to reclaim the limelight and now bursting for his place in the sun in this conversation, "have you seen my latest article?"

"No," acknowledged Mertens with a kind of indifference.

"I compare the Australian constitution with the Brazilian constitution. You know the Brazilian constitution is a beautiful document, a perfect document, but no one pays any attention to it because everyone in Brazil is corrupt, the executive, the judiciary... everyone."

"You can teach a comparative constitutional law subject when you teach in the Italian programme, yes?"

"Yes Noah." There was nothing more seductive to academics than the opportunity to teach overseas or to deliver a paper at an overseas conference. Francisco was salivating at the image of being one of the chosen few to teach in the Italian programme of intensive courses taught jointly by staff from the Besser block university and the historic university in Italy.

Lana was the guru of property law in the eyes of her colleagues in the law school of the Besser block university. This meant that she had edited a book on the topic in which she had written a single chapter and included the work of others in the remainder of her book. It was wonderful because she periodically updated material for the issue of the next edition. Each time she would include the book on her curriculum vitae and by about the fifth edition it appeared that she had written five books instead of just one chapter. She liked to promote the idea, despite the fact she had really only ever written one chapter within one book.

Lana had a certain way with people where she could dominate their thinking patterns to such an extent that they ceased to think logically. Some might have seen her as a dominating and manipulating personality, a person who was highly destructive of the anyone who got in her way. She had a way with men of which not even Mertens was aware.

Noah came across Lana one Saturday when she was in her office and he had just concluded a mooting meeting with his Vis team.

Noah thought he might flatter her to test her out. "You are showing uncommon dedication to be in here on a Saturday." The corridors of the law school were empty like the streets of Dodge city on a windy day. They were alone as Noah shut the door behind himself.

"Oh, it's you," said Lana almost deprecatingly. She liked to treat men as if they were mere objects, her subjects. As she swivelled around in her seat, Noah could see that she had those leather boots on. It was the boots that unleashed his lusting ways. What might happen was not his fault he resolved. *Women should not dress that way,* he thought. She pushed a chair in his direction directly opposite her and close. "Sit down." It was a command that Noah Mertens had no will to resist. As he sat down, her legs rubbed against his and she spread her dress to reveal the black panties beneath. *I could not say that she is beautiful, but her body is firm* he thought, and he could imagine certain things that were indeed about to happen.

"I want to go to Italy" declared Lana.

"Well, you know, you have to have a role there," replied Noah. "What role do you have in mind?"

"Perhaps I can lend you a hand."

"Well, to change my mind, perhaps a mouth could assist."

The deal was sealed by her lips as Lana leaned forward, a contract in lust. Noah knew there was a price to pay but, hey, you scratch my back, I will scratch yours was his creed. As long as he rewarded her, she would not create problems for him. That was his thought. He saw her as a scorpion, and a scorpion does not change its nature. He should have added something to this thought, perhaps 'nor does a dominatrix after she has turned the man into her slave.'

Several months later, law school staff duly filed into the staff room for a briefing by the dean. Mertens bounced into the room and at the appropriate moment reflected on the Italian programme which had just been completed.

"I am very pleased and proud to report that we have just returned from a very successful Italian programme up there in northern Italy. The Italian programme was an outstanding success. We had many cross-institutional enrolments. The university has made a lot of money out of the programme this year. And, it has created international opportunities for our students to study International Trade Law, European Union Law, and even comparative international constitutional law. I want to particularly thank Lana for her hard work and dedication to the task at hand." His thoughts turned back to the villa and the black leather worn by Lana, and he did not even mind her use of the strap on him. He just did not want his wife to see any of the healing welts. "You know actions speak louder than words, and we have succeeded beyond all expectations. This is because we aim for excellence, and excellence is open ended. We are simply the best."

When Nickie went to the coffee shop with Professor Francisco Kreuger, he discovered that Francisco had a version of the same problems that beset Dean Mertens. Francisco opened his wallet to find there was literally nothing in there. Not a dollar coin and not even a single note was present there. He apologised profusely in his charming Brazilian way and offered to not have anything at all.

"Don't worry Francisco. This one is on me."

Francisco sat at the table waiting for Nickie who duly appeared juggling two cups of coffee.

"Well," said Nickie, "welcome back from Italy." He paused momentarily before he continued. "Noah says it is the greatest programme we ever created so I expect it really was a success."

"Ugh! It was simply awful. Electricity in the town was frequently out. It was the middle of summer and the weather was really hot, and you could hardly breathe and none of the accommodation provided had air conditioning."

"So, apart from that the accommodation was generally acceptable?" Nickie queried.

'Acceptable?" echoed Francisco, "it was a nightmare. Honestly, I tell you Nickie. It was a basement. It was underground. One day I bought all this food at the market and struggled back with bags of shopping. I put it in the refrigerator. And then there was a blackout. Because the unit was underground, I could not see anything. Not even the hand in front of my face. I had to crawl along the wall to find my way. I lost all of the food. It was a disaster!"

"How did Noah react to the accommodation?" asked Nickie.

"He stayed in a beautiful villa with Lana."

"With Lana? Really? Did she have a role there?"

"No," said Francisco. "She did nothing. Just sightseeing. Oh, and she insulted Professor Lorenzo Carbona. Well, she said terrible things about the Catholic Church and Lorenzo is a devout Catholic. He did not want to talk to her after that."

"What about Mertens? Could you speak to him about this?"

"He left early and went to teach in Paris. Then he taught an intensive somewhere else in Europe and I never saw him until I got back here."

"Francisco, when he stayed in Italy was his wife with him?"

"No."

"Oh."

Was there anything between them? This was the question he longed to ask Francisco, but he hesitated, and the moment was gone. In light of Lana's propensity to wear leather and her general bullish tendency to be outspoken, Nickie began to wonder about the relationship between his honourable dean and this brash, ill-mannered woman.

Chapter 8
The Weakest Link

Danny Duval was a natural mooter, persuasive, authoritative, calm under pressure and low key in a very respectful way. He had the manner of a man who wanted to work with the tribunal, and assist it to see the correct law and the right interpretation of the vexed issues before it.

He moved into summary mode in the practice moot as he reached the conclusion of his case.

"By way of summary, the tribunal has jurisdiction to hear this dispute under the 'kompetenz-kompetenz' doctrine and under both the applicable arbitration rules and the UNCITRAL model law. Second, the so-called condition precedent in clause 5 is unenforceable because of its vagueness and uncertainty and, in any event, the respondent waived its right to conciliate.

"On the merits we have argued that the respondent must pay damages for the following reasons. First; under the UNIDROIT principles, second; the existence of a contract of sale which they have breached, third; the agreed terms are the contract, and the standard terms are replaced by virtue of the 'knock-out-doctrine' which invalidates the respondent's exclusion clause. Finally, there is an entitlement to damages under Article 7 point 4 point 1 of the PICC.

"Unless the tribunal has any further questions, this concludes the claimant's case."

Mertens kept everyone waiting before he finally looked up from the notes he had in front of him. "You still need a 'big bang' case theory to conclude on. A summary is okay, but it is boring. You need to lift up the Tribunal and to make your case inviolable."

Mertens paused again. "Before we conclude and have our piece of cake, you have to tell me one last thing. Tell me, who is the weakest link in the team and why? And tell me why you should be oralist and not the others."

"We are a team professor. We like each other. We support each other."

"I will give each of you a moment, and then I will nominate. If you wish to stay on this team you will give me an answer."

Chrissie had an idea and she knew it would almost certainly fail the Mertens test, but she could not help herself. She had to try it even if he sacked her.

"Yes, that's right Dean Mertens. It is hard for us. I nominate myself as the weakest link. I try hard but I am not as good an oralist as the others."

"Nonsense!" responded Noah who was beginning to enjoy watching the students squirm.

Breaking the ranks Alex declared, "I think Linda is the weakest link." In order to cover his tracks, he decided to sugar coat his disloyalty by adding with feigned sincerity, "She is an excellent researcher, but not such a great oralist. This is not to say she is bad. She is very competent, but it is just not her thing."

"All right, you have said enough. I agree with Alex," said Linda, jumping under the bus for the sake of the team.

The pain just grew and grew for the students who had not expected to be pitted against each other, and who genuinely liked each other. But they were competitive lawyers in the making, and the dark side beckoned. Noah at last was enjoying the session. He was a King and Queen maker and with any luck some easy sex might come his way in the near future. The girls were beautiful.

When at last it was time for the cake, Noah was positively salivating for the taste of his sinful pleasures. He was a magician and he was also so devilishly smart. He was the best when only the best will do, simply the best.

That night, after the shark attack, and frenzy of self-examination and examination of their friends, as the team was packing up to leave, Danny looked up at Mertens with a slight look of desperation.

"Professor do we really need to bring cakes to every meeting? I struggle with my budget and would rather go without cake to buy essential things."

"What?" exploded Mertens. "Every team I have has cake. We always have cake. That is how we bond." He paused to wipe a crumb from his face. "We always have cake. That will not change."

The students quickly finished assembling their things and said their goodbyes. They fled into the night with a sense of collective relief. The night of forced betrayal was over at last! In any event, the competition was only a few weeks away, and it would soon all be over.

They duly flew out to the circuit of pre-moots that led into the main competition in Vienna. In Ghent in Belgium, before the pre-moot competition there, the team practised against a Japanese team. Mertens looked very happy at its conclusion. When he joined the team for the taxi ride back to their hotel, he was carrying a brown paper bag.

"Did they pack you a lunch in that?" asked Alex bemused by such a learned professor carrying what looked like a school lunch.

"No, no just some sushi. You know the Japanese. They always have to offer something."

"Oh."

'They weren't very good at answering questions, were they?"

"Their primary submissions were okay," said Alex.

"Their law was good," chimed in Linda.

'You cannot say to them that they are crap," said Mertens, "when it comes to answering questions. They never go anywhere in this moot because their English is never quite good enough. They do not have a question bank. They do not do what they should do to compensate for their marginal English. They never make it through to the knockout rounds."

"Professor, how do they go with their scholarship?"

"Sometimes very good. They can sometimes receive Highly Commended awards for their Memoranda. That is their high water mark and it only happens once every five or six years."

When the taxi arrived back at the hotel, Mertens fled without a word, and the students fumbled for euros to pay the taxi driver. This would not be the first time that they would be left to pay.

In Vienna it soon became obvious to the team that their learned coach was not keen to pay for anything in particular. He developed the secret of invisibility when it came to bills. He was always somewhere else, like at the rest room or proclaiming that he would find the table while they ordered and paid for the coffee and cake. There was always cake. The evening meals, when they were not provided by some function or other, were always left to the students to pay. It was as if Mertens was not receiving a healthy living allowance, or in possession of the law school credit card or a dean's salary. But perhaps he was saving that all up for some other purpose. At the functions associated with the moot, Mertens would commandeer a tray of food or a tray of wine and champagne shamelessly from waiters who must have shuddered when they saw him coming. A feeding frenzy would follow when at least the students might be able to consume a morsel or two left over by the insatiable dean.

In Vienna, the oralists were Fiona (Fifi) and Danny.

Working quietly in their shared room, Danny opened up to Alex.

"My money is completely gone. I am out of money. Can you give me a loan?"

"I'm not in great shape myself. Why don't you borrow some money from Mertens? You can pay him back later."

Danny was not so sure. "He can be very unsympathetic."

"Surely he can respond and show some basic humanity," responded Alex.

"Okay. We'll see."

The walk along the corridor was long and Danny felt ill at ease about asking for help, but everything told him that he had to do so.

"Can I see you about something?"

"Yes, yes of course. Come in," invited Mertens.

"Professor, there have been a lot of expenses and I have run out of money. I wondered if I could borrow around a hundred euros from you. I can pay you back as soon as we return to Australia. I would be really grateful if you could."

"No," replied Mertens forcefully, "it is not in your interest for me to lend you money."

"But Professor, if I do not have money, I cannot eat."

"If you are hungry you will moot better." Mertens stood, moved towards the door and opened it for Danny to leave.

The sadness Danny felt extrapolated into a flat performance the next day. He mooted well as he always did because, if nothing else, he was exceptionally well drilled in the craft of mooting. However, the wallet of good fortune was empty, and the team was narrowly defeated in a close decision.

"That was a disgustingly poor performance. You were mediocre," said Mertens, "you can find your own way back to the hotel."

The night of the awards they did manage to achieve a Highly Commended Respondent memorandum and Fifi was acknowledged also with a Highly Commended Oralist award. They were not best memorandum or best oralist but still substantial achievements. But there was still an emptiness in the pit of the stomach for members of the team. They sampled a little too much of the free champagne and the wheat beer and then headed out on to the streets. They were exploring and didn't really quite know or care where they were.

"Hey, where's Fiona, I mean Fifi?" asked Danny.

After an awkward pause Linda responded. "Oh, she's meeting Noah… for a debriefing."

"I reckon she'll be the one who is de-briefed all right by Herr Professor," said Rebel with a note of harshness in her voice.

The excessive alcohol consumed had really loosened Alex's tongue. "Ze Fuhrer has spoken. You vill take off zee pants unt der bustenhalter unt you vill kneel to zee great one."

"He offers incentives, and he has the power to make things happen," said Rebel.

"The great aphrodisiac!" exclaimed Chrissie out of nowhere.

Alex sang mimicking the words of a song by Kasey Chambers in a little girl voice, or as close to that as he could come in his drunken state. "Am I not pretty enough? Do I not moot well enough?"

"Ain't it a shame I can't research," joined in Linda.

"Don't you know it makes me feel so sad," squeezed in Chrissie.

"Am I not difficult enough," sang Linda.

"Can I not pay the bill any more," joined in Danny.

"Am I not pretty enough?" chorused Linda.

"Thank God you're not the favoured one," added Chrissie in a note of finality.

They were now on the waterfront and Danny raced ahead along a narrow jetty to where some sailing boats were moored.

"You are all crap. This moot is crap. The judges are crap. Everyone is crap, except me the great law dean. 'Look on thy works ye mighty and despair'." Danny loosened a boat from its mooring, and Alex did the same. Then he jumped on board a boat and foraged through a cupboard to find some china plates.

"This is what I think of you. Here, have a plate. You will moot better if you are hungry!" Thus saying, he threw a plate hard onto the wooden floor of the boat. Alex jumped down and grabbed a few plates and distributed them to Chrissie and Linda and Rebel. They all stood in a line and called out loudly "You are crap!" and with this they each threw the plates vigorously onto the floor of the jetty smashing them into pieces in the process.

"We had better go before we are arrested," said Linda as the least drunk one in the team.

"Yeah, let's go," said Alex, who wanted a career in the law rather than behind bars. Even in his drunken state he realised the need to get away from there and pushed Danny back onto the pier and they all started to run as best they could which was not necessarily in a straight line or without falling down several times.

When the boys woke in their shared room the next day, they did not feel exactly chipper. There were groans and then suddenly Danny sat up in his bed.

"What did we do last night?" asked Danny with great seriousness.

"Well… er… you freaked out. Don't you remember?" responded Alex, who had advanced survival skills when it came to himself and his own involvement in things.

"I just remember broken plates," said Danny.

"We did some damage down by the waterfront. I think we need to get ready to catch that plane and the sooner we get out of here the better."

"My head feels like a pumpkin," groaned Danny as he began to move.

During the flight home, the team was very quiet. The weeks and months of hard work, and the nervous exhaustion from competition had finally taken its toll on them. Although air flight is not conducive to sleep for many, this time around all members took time to rest and sleep. They didn't have to worry about Dean Mertens as he was travelling first class, and they were travelling economy, and they had managed to leave the country without being arrested. They were relieved on that count and regretful for their actions. Their love for their distinguished coach was gone forever. Fifi hoped that her lies about what she and Mertens did to debrief would be believed.

Back in Australia at the Besser block university Mertens spoke glowingly at the next law school functions, and put a positive gloss on the team's performance. They quickly returned to their studies and study mode and, for them, the mooting experience was very 'over'. What happened when they were away, stayed their little secret.

After an alumni function, at which Noah made yet another great speech in praise of himself, he and visiting dean, Dr Andreas Hoffmann, a former German academic, were joined for dinner at a city restaurant by

Francisco Kreuger. Although Francisco was Brazilian, his family were German immigrants who had settled initially in the township of Petropolis in Brazil. Both Mertens and Hoffmann had already consumed a substantial volume of alcohol when they sat down for their dinner, and of course they needed to order more. They quickly ordered more champagne for Mertens and more red wine for Hoffmann.

"I do not have a research assistant," lamented Francisco. "It makes life very hard, hard to produce as many articles as I would like. I could do so much more if there were more money directed into providing research."

"You should think more global and seek out research grants and projects. You are international, aren't you?"

"Well I come from Brazil, but I completed my PhD in this country and my work is loved overseas, but not so much in Australia."

"It is so much easier with research money," said Hoffmann. "I have several national grants and many researchers. I have so many minions that it is very easy for me to be very productive."

"I have more slaves than you." Mertens was indeed grumpy and not to be exceeded by this German upstart. "How many slaves do you have to make you look good?"

"Mmm I have five at my university."

"Only five," scoffed Mertens. "You have to be joking. You are an amateur. I have at least five at my university, but I have several others at other universities that exclusively co-author with me. And I have one slave who more or less works for me full-time writing articles. I have research power."

"Well, if you are talking international," responded Hoffmann, "I have many more than that. I have at least another five in Germany, who are completing both research papers and articles on research grant moneys, and I have a slave in Singapore. So I have many more than you."

"Well, I even have slaves in China," responded Mertens who was confident in his numbers and, if they were not enough, he could invent some more. He was confident of outnumbering or outboasting his German colleague. He had to win, and he would win. Truth was not in his lexicon anyway, so he was uninhibited.

Francisco sat back watching this boasting match go on, and wondering about the values or the sense of shame or humility that these scholars should have been exhibiting. As they became louder and more extravagant in their claims, he noticed other diners at adjoining tables giving them dirty looks as if they wanted them to stop being so loud and so obnoxious. These reactions, of course, would have been lost on these two senior scholars each bathing in the glory of their own magnificence like two giant gorillas asserting territorial rights.

"No one has more than me. I have slaves in universities all around Australia and in Italy and Belgium and Germany and France. You cannot compete with me. I am the slave master, the King of all slaves."

"Well I am a God, and have more minions than you can count."

"You are just another pagan. God is on my side. I am a Roman Catholic and I go to church. Catholics can do anything and everything! We are untouchable."

"That's the problem with Catholics. They think they can do anything, and they are still good, still forgiven. The problem with the world today is Catholics. I admit it." He gathered himself together for one final concession. "You have more Catholics than I have slaves."

Francisco failed to follow the logic of the conversation. He could see they were both in a very drunken state.

"I am the slave master!" asserted Mertens.

Hoffmann was quiet and Francisco knew that Mertens always had to have the last word.

"I think it is time to get you two king makers to your home or hotel room," said Francisco. "I will get the car and meet you out front."

Francisco paused for a moment, and then thought he had to say this to ensure it happened. He knew he simply could not afford to pay. His wallet was almost empty once again, and he had left his credit card at home deliberately.

"Don't forget to pay the bill."

Mertens warned the staff at the staff meeting. "The university requires me to complete a performance review on every member of staff. I will circulate an email to everyone and ask for you to indicate a couple of times when you are available, and we can firm up appointments for this evaluation. You must treat this seriously because the Kremlin are keen to cut off unproductive staff. So you must record all of your publications. Provide the information asked for in the emails and then, when we meet, we can explore ways to improve productivity, especially when it comes to writing articles, scholarly articles. We are helped greatly by the number of articles published in A- and A-plus journals by Francisco and myself, but the performance seems to drop off after that. So I need you to help me by submitting your updated CV and a list of your publications over the last three years." He paused. "If you don't help me, I cannot help you."

The performance appraisal process was a box-ticking exercise but, where most of the staff at the Besser block university had been there for some considerable time and managed to get away with doing very little work for their salary, there was inertia and more, much more.

Sandra Wallis sat before Mertens in his office. He had the big chair. She had the small chair. He liked his accoutrements.

"Sandra, I see that you have written only one or two articles in the last twelve years. Could you have been more productive?"

"I had a lot going on. I have been heavily involved with academic feminist issues, and there has just not been the time. I also edit a Law Journal and that takes a lot of time."

"Yes, but I notice that you haven't published a single issue in the last two years. Why was that?"

The tears began to flow like wine from Sandra's eyes. Her marital problems, her student complaint problems, her martyrdom for the cause of gender equality, her treatment by generations of deans and how hard she works all flowed amidst a backdrop of copious tears. Even Mertens, who had a substantial track record as a misogynous academic, found himself offering succour and reassurance for someone he really did not like. He duly patted her on the shoulder, and emphasised the need to write more articles.

Raphael Chevrolet, when he sat in front of Mertens, conveyed a sense of confidence. "I think," he said, "that my publications record is very strong, and this is reflected by my curriculum vitae list of publications. It is very substantial."

"Yes," said Noah as he looked Raphael directly in the eyes, "but in all you have only really written two or three articles. You keep re-writing the introduction and leaving the rest the same, and for some they are just translations of the same articles in two or three languages." Noah paused. "You realise that I am a European and I can speak most of these languages."

"I also had my research assistant look at your list, and for ranking purposes, it is rather hard for us because you have that tendency to publish a paper in one language, and then to rename it and publish it in a different language. As I said you re-jig existing publications and re-title them and publish them in another country."

"Well I admit that I do a lot of work for the United Nations. I have world expertise in my specialty and need to disseminate my material widely. I am an internationalist."

"Look, all this," declared Mertens with a sense of largesse that he could now afford to exercise, "is our little secret." Like a benevolent godfather he leaned forward and said, "At some point I may need a favour."

When Associate Professor Gary Worth took his seat for the performance appraisal, he was quickly into stride, seizing the initiative instantly from Mertens.

"There is something we need to discuss."

"That is what we are here for, performance appraisal."

"No, I do not mean that."

Noah's mouth dropped, as he was simply not used to being subject to another person. This was his show, and he thought in his mind loud thoughts of anger. However, as he began to mouth a response, Gary leapt forward.

"There is a need for another professorship in this law school."

"Yes, I agree," echoed Mertens. "As we grow so should we attract outstanding scholars, and the best way of doing that initially, is to create another professorship."

"I think that we should look to recognise someone in the law school who already has the credentials for such an appointment and that is me."

"You?" responded Mertens with a sense of surprise and bewildered amazement, akin to that of Walter Pidgeon when he exclaimed "Sunny Tufts!".

"I have an important profile that is recognised at national level. My article on restorative justice was widely read and is very influential. I am the best you have, and you will lose credibility if you do not promote or appoint me at professorial level."

Mertens did not like to be the one squirming and swallowing his words, but this was self-delusion operating at its highest level. Noah decided to meet fire with fire.

"I understand you have made a contribution, but your publications profile barely justifies your current ranking of Associate Professor. Your last five or six articles have been jointly authored."

"I was the dominant author."

"Your name is not listed first," said Mertens, "and, in any event, they were only published in B-ranked journals... B-ranked journals! You have no chance of promotion unless you publish substantially in A- or A-plus ranked journals. That is the name of the game."

"I am offended at your attitude. How could you possibly consider that anyone else would have a better record? This exercise is a charade and an insult to me! I have better things to do. Good day!" Without further ado, Gary stomped from the room and out into the corridor slamming the door behind him and making his way to his desk in his room beyond that.

"We'll see about this," he muttered.

As Nickie walked down the corridor towards his performance review appraisal, he passed Danny Duval walking down the corridor in the other direction.

Nickie nodded, and recalling the recent successes of the Vis team in Vienna, he felt moved to comment.

"Congratulations on the moot result!"

"For what?" snapped Danny, and he was gone before he could be pressed for further explanation. The smile on Nickie's face turned to a look of concern. He knew there was more to know, that the reports yet again had distorted the truth of the matter. *How easily does the sage academic lie,* he thought, as he made his way to the cusp of his performance review interview with his august dean.

Chapter 9
Making One's Way

Nickie thought back to when he initially accepted the position at the Besser block university. He remembered the time when he and Will sat down in the coffee shop in the sandstone university's main quadrangle. It was then that Nickie announced his news.

"Well, I am leaving."

"Has he finally got around to kicking you out too?" queried Will.

"No," said Nickie, "I have jumped. Noah Mertens faxed an offer to me yesterday and I accepted it. So I am westward bound... very soon."

"Did he give you a promotion?"

"Yes, one level higher."

"When are you leaving and how soon?"

"Very soon. If I had my way, by yesterday. I shall miss some of the office staff and a few of my colleagues, but the writing is on the wall. A period of attrition followed by a new-look law school focusing on the tunnel vision of what a law school should look like in the eyes of our glorious dean."

"Are you sure you know what you are getting into by going with Mertens? He has a reputation for financial irresponsibility and selfishness."

"No, I do not definitely know what is in store for me under Mertens. I know he is an alpha male type and always wants to be right, even if he is wrong. I just hope, somehow I can make a contribution there, as I surely cannot contribute here. Who knows what the future holds?"

"Amen," added Will.

"Oh, by the way, how are you going to get there. You know Perth is the most isolated capital city in the world. I presume you are flying, or do you have no sense?"

"Yes," smiled Nickie, "I have no sense. We are driving."

"I don't know if you are brave or foolhardy."

Chapter 10
The Nullarbor Plain

The early days in the car were relatively predictable. To shorten the journey, Nickie and Bianca took the inland route right across the state of New South Wales to the township of Broken Hill. Broken Hill is a mining town associated with films like *Mad Max 2* and *Wake in Fright*. A one night's dalliance was all the time he could afford, before moving on to tackle the Nullarbor Plain. The greatest memory he had, apart from kangaroos and a fox he saw along the way, was the extent of road-kill, the wildlife struck down by cars. They signalled the need for care in driving, and to not continue driving into the night.

The Nullarbor, as it is locally called, was supposed to be a particularly arid area and indeed there were great expanses of treeless plain, and a road that snaked out of sight. The road across the Nullarbor is the longest, straightest and flattest road in the country. The drive across the Nullarbor is around 1,700km in length. There was no question about driving all the way non-stop for on this route it is foolhardy in the extreme to contemplate driving after dark. That is, unless you are prepared to play Russian roulette with the wildlife, namely, huge kangaroos that can suddenly leap into the path of your vehicle at dawn or at dusk, or in the night, or families of emus that can wander across the road at any time, and snakes that can be flung up into the wheel housing of your vehicle creating a dangerous, poisonous time-bomb, waiting silently to strike down the weary driver at the next roadhouse stop.

Before leaving South Australia to navigate the Nullarbor, Nickie and Bianca stayed at the motel in Ceduna, which was a beautiful seaside township of just over 2000 citizens. Nickie was surprised that the township's motel was surrounded by a large wire fence. He presumed it was to protect the motel from intrusion by that part of the local indigenous population, which gambled and drank itself into acts of violence and burglary late at night. He had never experienced a township divided by race, and he was sure he must be somehow wrong in detecting a divide within the community living in this remote, but idyllic environment. He did not trust his instincts in this place, as his perception was superficial, based on one night. At the same time as allowing that his perceptions may be wrong, he felt sad at the thought of such divisions existing (if his imagined thoughts were anywhere near the truth). He recalled his many indigenous students, and how brilliant in most cases these individuals were. He felt uncomfortable at the thought that a racial divide existed in such a racially diverse society. He felt it did and he felt sad that racism may be entrenched in parts of this country that he so loved.

The next night, after a long day of driving that took them into the great expanses of the Australian state of Western Australia, they stayed at a motel at a roadhouse. They were so grateful for a bed, a place to lay down in and stay the night, that nothing mattered to them save the opportunity to place the head on a pillow and to stretch out in comfort to embrace the waves of sleep that swept in.

Amazingly, as they began their drive across the Nullarbor Plain, a place of profound isolation and desert, the sky was overcast and drops of rain appeared on the windscreen of their car. Shortly, the rain drove down hard, and the windscreen wipers were on full power to create the vision needed to stay on the road and on track.

The rain continued on and off, until they pulled into a roadhouse in order to refuel, order a meal and bed down for the night in its motel part. The motel was rather tattered but the important parts of their room, like the bed, was clean and the shower and toilet worked so this was all that was needed. However, as a film buff, Nickie could not resist himself when he saw the layers of silt or dust on most things, the tattered and torn fly screen and the swimming pool that looked like it had not been in operation for decades. It was more like an overgrown sandpit, than a functioning or resting pool.

"Looks like I booked us into the Bates Motel," he said. "All we need now is Anthony Perkins and Grandma."

"Feel like a game of scrabble and some cheese?" asked Bianca.

Against all of Nickie's expectations, it rained throughout the night and next morning the car park looked more like the pool than the pool itself.

That day, when Nickie pulled the car off the main highway and drove a few hundred metres to a lookout, he felt humbled by the isolation of everything. Finally, he felt the pull of the continent. It was harsh, awe-inspiring, dangerous and beautiful, all at the one time. This was the obligatory photo stop to photograph the Great Southern Ocean, and the line of what looked like sandstone cliffs along the southern coast of Australia. Soon enough they arrived at the Besser block university in Perth, Western Australia.

As Nickie walked from the apartment on campus that he was temporarily staying in on the way to the law school, he noticed that the rabbits were out hopping around the ground areas finding things to nibble on. He also noticed the black cockatoos up high nibbling on nuts. Mostly, he kept his eyes on the ground after he saw the signs, multiple signs warning about the dangers presented by the poisonous dugite snakes that frequented the local bushland and could be found even very near to the buildings of the university. Thankfully, he saw none. He thought *I hope the snakes in the grass here are not the two-legged ones.*

The first thing Nickie noted about Mertens' room when he entered it, was its size. It was large, suitably grand for a law dean.

"It is better here," said Mertens, "it is better here than that other place," which was Noah Mertens' name for the sandstone university in the eastern state.

"Even the CBD is better than here," continued Mertens. "The shops are better. It is a better place. You will see."

"I want you," said Mertens, "to teach torts, and to create a moot court bench that we can use in our mooting programmes. "You know I will take a Vis team to Vienna. My teams always do very well."

"With the Moot Court Bench, you run it like we did in the other place. Once they are trained, the students on the MCB can be very useful to us. They can train the other students, run competitions. You can even take one or two into mooting teams. You will rapidly build up, and you know I expect nothing but the best."

"I imagine," replied Nickie, "that we can build a mooting culture within two or three years. Then I think we can start to win competitions."

Mertens seemed peeved at this thought. "No, we must win quickly. I want to point to success in our first year. We have the Vis, but you must also manufacture a win. We are the experienced coaches here. I need to be able to demonstrate success."

"Oh." Nickie could feel the screws tightening.

"How is your wife?"

"Not so good at the moment. She is out of her comfort zone," said Nickie. "New place, new challenges, knows no one, that kind of thing."

'Perhaps I can help."

"I don't know if I will like it here," announced Bianca when Nickie returned to the apartment on campus.

"Noah wants to know if you could do some part-time work, maybe for two or three days a week, in the law school office. I think he wants to get rid of Charlene, the office manager there, and he just wants to shore up numbers in the office staff. Are you interested? It would at least give you something to do which can always help when you are in a new city and do not know anyone."

"Yes, I would like that."

Alexia ('Lexie') Watson was one of the 'old guard'. She had been there almost from the beginning of the law school some ten years before. She grew up, in an academic sense, under conditions of student numbers and classes taught, that had long been superseded. The leisurely ways of the past and the beneficent workloads no longer existed. But somehow the original staff had managed to dominate and bully past deans into attempting to maintain the old workloads. As a consequence, there was a general reluctance to take on a more 'modern', more realistic workload as compared to the numbers of classes taught, the number of tutorials conducted, the number of research students supervised, and higher degree students supervised. The culture when it came to workload issues was saccharine due to the low workloads allocated in the early years as the school grew.

This is not to say that Lexie was a bully, merely that she was used to getting her way. When it came to the new dean, she did not really know how he operated but she was about to learn as she sat before him.

"What can I do for you?" asked Mertens although it sounded more like a command that a question.

"I have an opportunity," said Lexie. "I have been approached by the Port of Fremantle Collective to undertake research and write a report about the Port of Fremantle. As a maritime lawyer, I am well placed to undertake such enquiries and to make recommendations for the further development of the port and the legal regime applying to it."

"Can you not do this while you are performing your other duties?"

"No, no," said Lexie, "it is not possible. The project will take at least six months of my time. In order to complete it properly I will need to devote all of my time to it."

"No, it is out of the question. There is a financial squeeze on, and we need our more experienced teachers in the classrooms and lecture theatres."

"Perhaps I could buy in a replacement to give my lectures from the grant funds?" queried Lexie.

"This is out of the question. The pro-vice-chancellor was very definitive in his last meeting with the deans."

"Oh."

"Yes. He said that there is too much outside practice and that staff must be discouraged from neglecting their duties purely to earn money from outside bodies. Under current circumstances, I cannot approve your request.

"This Port of Fremantle Collective group, are they even in the phone book?" asked Mertens.

"No but they do have a website, which has quite a bit on it." Lexie wondered why he bothered to ask this question when he had already refused her request. Only later did she realise why he had posed the question.

Nickie came across Lexie in the corridor as she returned from the restroom, her eyes red as if she had shed a few tears. He followed her into her room and asked if she felt like a coffee. They repaired to the nearest coffee shop on campus, which also happened to be the student bar.

"I had a great opportunity to do a customised report into the effectiveness of the Port of Fremantle, and he won't let me do it. First, he denies me approval. Then he phones up the collective and offers to do the work himself."

"He didn't, did he?"

"Well you should know him. You worked with him before, didn't you?"

"Well, yes, he has an interesting background, but I always gave him the benefit of the doubt and now I must give loyalty to my dean, even if he is less than perfect."

"Then he asked his PA to check on funds available for employing research assistants. So he wants to do it and pocket all the grant money himself."

"Really," Nickie muttered, now lost in his own thoughts and sipping coffee to give himself time to think, telling himself not to react to Lexie's anger but to make up his own mind. He knew Mertens to be an alpha male but felt insecure about how well he really knew Mertens.

"Jack, our previous dean, would have allowed me to take the leave. But this dean … he's hard."

"Well," responded Nickie, "I know he doesn't like to be wrong. Even if he is in the wrong, he will still blame you. He concedes nothing. I just thought him to be a typical alpha male." *There I go,* he thought, *I've said too much again.*

Lexie was at her flash point, not sure if tears were coming or her tongue would be sharpened by her anger. "I thought he was supposed to be a leader not a deceiver."

"You're probably right but there can always be things we don't know about, that relate to outside practice. He may just be carrying out other's policy. At some universities they have outside practice units that monitor and strictly control outside work and you have to share any income with the university."

"I think he's a pig!" Lexie exclaimed with passion and emotion.

"He does have a vision for the law school. He is imperfect. On the other hand, I have seen a lot worse."

"You're just too nice," said Lexie.

"Time will tell, I suppose." Nickie was fighting his own negativity at this stage of the conversation and rapidly made an excuse of needing to go back to the books to prepare the next lecture.

For Nickie the law school was far too quiet in the evenings. On some nights it was like one of those American ghost towns from the wild west. Nickie half expected a spinifex ball to roll down the deserted corridors. This night there were students in the building in the Law Students Society room downstairs from the main staff corridor. And upstairs there was only Nickie working away quietly on his lecture materials. A strong wind outside rattled the windows and door frames and hummed down the corridor.

Nickie was in deep concentration on his lectures this particular night. He liked to perfect them a week in advance which meant producing PowerPoints which he used to carry some of the detail. They also provided the structure of the lecture, and an opportunity to lift the lecture above the mundane through the addition of visuals, backgrounds of judges and quotations from cases and commentators. He was lost in concentration and then, suddenly, his concentration was broken by raucous noises from the ground floor, yahoo-ing, chanting and clapping which was so loud it echoed up the corridor. His curiosity aroused, Nickie walked out to the balcony from which he could see most of the foyer. A feature of the foyer was the big couches that were spread around it for the comfort of students waiting to enter the big lecture theatre located off it.

As Nickie walked closer, the urging on and clapping and overall noises grew louder and louder until, now at the edge of the balcony, he could see what was going on. There was a group of drunken students surrounding one of the couches on which a male student was having intercourse with a female student. Nickie saw himself as liberal, but not so much so as to countenance such behaviour. But he felt that he was too new on the ground to do anything in particular about it. He just hoped that security might arrive and bring the offending behaviour to a close and he toyed with the idea of phoning them. He was shocked by the debauched goings-on. *What a culture!* he thought.

"What is the student culture like here?" Nickie asked Mertens when they next met.

Avoiding the issue, Mertens answered, "It will be good. I have given them rooms and one I took from the Feminist Lawyers Association. I offered them some money to leave and they took it.

"The students here love me, and I can trick the university. I put money into a special account held by the Law Students' Association, and it does not come up on university accounts. When I have a mooting bill to pay I simply tell them, and they pay from the money I have hidden there. And I also give them money from this account to pay for their social activities. It works out well for everyone, so the Law Student's Association are important to me, to maintain good relations."

Nickie wanted to rejoin, by saying, 'Well I am not so keen on financing their sexual relations,' but he was afraid that he might feel the wrath of the dean if he did. So he stayed quiet for the time being. Instead he asked a question. He had his idea of the student culture, but he wanted to hear from his learned dean.

In the end Nickie could not restrain himself. "But Noah, is it not a corrupted culture that we are dealing with? We have to create a new culture, and it may take a few years depending upon how Neanderthal they are."

Mertens moved uncomfortably as Nickie offered up his insight. "No, not a few years. We can do it straight away. I want success. I demand success from you, from everyone. We have good relations with the student association. I scratch their back. They scratch my back. They will be helpful." He paused then concluded "It works well for everyone."

"So who is to be the first Chief Justice of the Moot Court Bench?"

"Sarah, Sarah Conners is our inaugural Chief Justice of the MCB," said Nickie.

"Yes, she is a little naïve, but she will do. There is not a lot of talent to work with at this stage. In the future we will make our own talent."

"When will the internal mooting competition take place?" asked Mertens.

"Well, er, I really haven't had a chance to think about it," responded Nickie.

"Is there no competition already in place?"

"Yes, I think they have something but now we have a moot court bench you can take it over. You should organise something straight away."

Mertens' personal assistant appeared at the door and their meeting dissolved, as Mertens had a phone call to make.

Within a day Nickie found himself sitting in a room with Sarah Conners and Eliot Drew, who was a rather unshaven, scruffily dressed president of the Law Students' Association.

"We would like to help you," said Nickie, "by running the internal mooting competition for you. We can provide a problem and the judges from the MCB and a few lecturers and make things a lot easier for you."

"No," announced Eliot, "we do it. We organise the internal mooting problem. We get sponsorship from a law firm which pays for our social programme and we have an active social programme. There is no way we would ever give it up."

"We can certainly assist you," said Sarah, already overstepping the mark in Nickie's eyes.

Nickie was taken aback by the pure naked aggression of Eliot, not so much by his words as by his demeanour, the naked aggression and the prejudicial attitude held by Eliot. He was not on board the Mertens train although he had some kind of arrangement with Mertens.

"All right, we will help you, but it is my belief that this job is done best by a Moot Court Bench. It is part of its core role. Let's talk again next year. We will go it alone and run our own competition if agreement is not reached at that time."

"Tell me," said Nickie, "have the students here competed in any international mooting competitions… of which you are aware?"

"No, but we compete in the ALSA moot every year," said Eliot.

"Do you have coaches?" asked Nickie, striving to be polite but not within himself feeling very polite in his emotions.

"No, we coach ourselves."

"Have you ever won?"

"No but we always have a good time."

"Oh."

"Yes, we do it our way," said Eliot, feeling aggressive again.

Nickie could feel himself descending into the labyrinth of student misconceptions and a student culture rooted in booze drinking, living in an infernal place where hard work and discipline were unwanted, rejected as being valueless sacrifice and where the dream of excellence could not survive the selfish, boorish, cynical values of the collective. He felt he could change this, but it would be a battle for years. And Mertens wanted him to change this corrupt culture overnight or did he really? Nickie felt restless and uneasy.

To a universal reaction of dismay, Noah Mertens announced at the next staff meeting that there would only be five tutorials offered in each of the core Bachelor of Laws subjects.

"We simply have not been given enough money by the central administration, who I call the Kremlin, to be able to sustain our tutorial programmes. It is something that I cannot help. They have cut our budget by 30%."

Audible groans were heard around the room until Lexie spoke up. "I thought we made money for the university. We do not have laboratories or expensive facilities, why?"

Wringing his hands, Mertens enjoyed playing the aggrieved dean.

"It has always been the case that the law school subsidises other parts of the university, the arts, where key subjects no longer attract enrolments, and also the veterinary school, which for a university of this size, eats up large amounts of the university's budget. It is a big, black hole that we keep alive by attracting students to study law. We pay for them all, but there is no justice. We are the first ones to be squeezed when the Kremlin needs money. I do not like it at all, and I argue strenuously against it, but it is the way of the world. We carry the load of the world on our shoulders."

As the staff meeting concluded, people emptied from the room leaving only Mertens and Nickie.

"Do you want to see me now?" asked Nickie.

"Yes, yes" said Mertens enthusiastically. "But first, was I good?"

"Yes, you were excellent, your usual excellent self." Nickie felt diminished by the question, and by his own answer, but he gave Mertens the answer he was seeking.

"I have to tell you," said Mertens, "I will be going to Sydney this weekend to attend the Futures Conference there. You will have to be acting dean in my absence. You do nothing. My PA does most of the work. You just sign what she tells you to sign. You will have to attend next week the university's 2020 meeting run by Gary Olds and the financial controller Ian Parker."

Once you reach a certain age, Nickie thought, time has a habit of rushing by you at an ever-increasing speed. Nickie had a sense of dread about this meeting since the moment he learnt he would be in the law school hot seat in the eyes of the university. Marnie did not seem to have any documents on the upcoming meeting when Nickie initially approached her. Eventually she produced an agenda on the cusp of the meeting.

Nickie soon found himself sitting at a very large round table. Garry Olds looked like a young executive, someone who somehow looked like a 'wanna be' as the Australians would call it. He wore the requisite blue suit and a power tie. Nickie thought that he looked out of place, like some kind of prissy real estate salesman about to make a pitch to a rich developer. Nickie thought there must surely be a Lamborghini or 'Merc' or BMW sitting in his garage.

Nickie felt genuinely anxious about this meeting. With no time and little knowledge at his disposal he was concerned that it may prove to be a trap for him, that his lack of preparation would be exposed.

Gary Olds leaned forward and grasped the microphone. "Now we need each department head to identify themselves and to give us an overview of how their department is meeting the goals set out in the university 2020 document. We can start with the traditional faculties. Let's kick the ball off with the law school. Who is here for them?"

"That's me. Nickie Jones standing in for Noah Mertens Dean of Law. I attend as acting dean in Professor Mertens' absence overseas." Nickie knew that he had his back to the wall, no knowledge, no briefing, no hope. Internally he was squirming, wishing he was not there at all.

"Well the law school is in a process of regeneration under Professor Mertens' leadership. It has added vitality to its publications profile by reactivating all of its journals with imminent deadlines for production of new editions. While we encourage staff to publish outside in A- and A-plus journals, these journals represent opportunities for staff to increase their output. They are refereed journals of quality. Additionally, we are reshaping the internal culture to provide students with opportunities to achieve measurable excellence through participation in international mooting competitions. These will represent a dynamic improvement in the profile and reputation of the law school." Nickie wondered if the audience was swallowing his verbose attempt to stall. He soon knew they were not. He just hoped they were not desirous of crucifying him on the spot.

"That's all very well," said Olds, "but what about the KPI of retention rates? This is a critical KPI to support the financial stability and development of the university."

"Well we do have a few problems with some of our part-timers dropping out, and varying retention rates as between core and optional subjects. We do find, sadly, that some first-year students simply cannot cope with the rigour required to succeed in the study of law. When they realise this, they discontinue. I think the law of torts last time around had a failure rate of twenty percent. We work hard on laying down a strong foundation of knowledge and skills for the study of law. Internally, we accept that, with all the good will in the world, it is not possible to push through students that the industry will reject as being incapable. For the sake of the discipline's long-term future, it is not possible to make it easier for students to progress."

Olds seemed out of sorts, uncharacteristically angry, but somehow, he kept himself quiet. However, the collective was not done with Nickie's doodling just yet. At such events there is always a pro-vice-chancellor charged with responsibility for teaching and learning.

A woman's voice pierced the quiet. Like an arrow her words raced towards Nickie.

"What has the law school done in terms of innovative teaching practices? Do you have mooks or flipped classrooms? Or is your delivery of lectures as it always had been?"

"Well, in answer to your question," said Nickie wondering at the same time about what he might say and how deep might be the hole he was digging for himself in Mertens' absence, "we have not yet embraced Moocs. We do not really have either the desire or the staff free to create them. And some of us see the flipped classroom concept as not relevant to our lectures which we give in traditional mode but hopefully with some creativity. Perhaps we should consider a variation of it for tutorials although, because of the mooting structure we may be engaged as judges, which takes our full focus, making it impossible to separately respond to questions while we are actually doing something else."

Olds tried one last time to move this recalcitrant law school in the direction of compliance.

"The flipped classroom has become a hallmark of teaching and learning at this university. Science has made a lot of it by integration it into their programmes... architecture also. Law should move in this direction."

Nickie was taking no prisoners, but he had a strong feeling of being ill-at-ease as he responded. Was he alienating everyone at the meeting? From his perspective he wondered about the extent to which they were all shareholders in the company, in a manner of speaking. He wondered if he was committing career suicide by voicing his real feelings. He wondered whether or not he was wise in giving in to his inner feelings and thoughts.

"As a traditional discipline, it is rather hard for us to embrace the flipped classroom where the students ask questions that show up on the lecturer's screen while the lecture is going on and the lecturer answers them instantly." He paused for a brief moment before he plunged back into the whirlwind. "For us it is virtually impossible to put this into practice. A law lecture carries a great deal of cerebral content, and it is not possible for us to convey that content while simultaneously answering questions on the computer screen, questions that might, for example, relate to something said ten minutes earlier. In our discipline we can innovate easier in other ways, for example, by incorporating mooting structures into our tutorial programme. We will continue to examine the flipped classroom concept, but, unless science is able to clone our lecturers, they will always struggle to do two separate tasks at the one time."

By now Olds had had enough of Nickie. He moved on to the veterinary school, a torch bearer for the university. Sympathetic smiles shone from the faces of those present. Nickie felt that their collective body language was along the lines of their thinking, *Yes, this is going to be good news. It is the vet school, our little darling.*

Nickie was relieved to surrender the spotlight and internally wriggled in his seat. He was desirous of being somewhere else, anywhere else. Nickie did not share overwhelming joy when he thought of the university's much celebrated vet school. He saw it as a place that benefitted from the cross funding provided at the expense of monies brought into the university by the law school, whose programmes were always popular but inexpensive to offer, whereas veterinary science required ongoing substantial amounts of capital, more than could come from its students' fees.

From the moment he stopped speaking Nickie was mentally out of the room. He wore a face that suggested he might be listening, or he might not be listening. He tried to go within himself into his own world that could not be touched by the university's psychotic emphasis on making money, or its focus on the dogma of education. He felt like a rebel but tried hard to sublimate his real feelings about how power was exercised. When the meeting did eventually come to a conclusion, he found himself fleeing as soon as the opportunity arose.

Later that afternoon, Nickie was still in his room working hard on researching for an article on the recent DVT litigation in the USA and in Australia. Although he was concluding that attempts to argue DVT cases in aviation law were close to useless, except, arguably, in very limited circumstances, he wanted to draw a line under the DVT litigation era once and for all time. He found the need to print out onto a printer in the photocopier/supplies room.

He was in process of collating and stapling the copies he had printed out when Lana bustled into the room. This was unusual. She preferred to use her office in out of school hours rather than when very many people were around. She was dressed as usual in her habitual dark-coloured clothing.

"What are you doing?" she asked pointedly.

With all the research, Nickie was feeling mentally jaded. "Oh, err... just researching and writing an article on DVT on long-haul flights."

"I wouldn't do too much research in that area. You know that they are cutting your subject as of next year."

"What?" Like a lemming heading towards the cliff, Nickie had taken the bait.

"Yes, they are cutting the electives as of next semester. Money is tight. Your subject will be axed."

In an instant she had gone. If true, she had smashed Nickie's hopes of establishing a dynasty of teaching aviation law, and possibly space law as well. In an instant Nickie felt a surge of anger that he just had to express but Lana was gone so he had no one to vent to. His victim became the door to the photocopier room as he slammed it with all the strength and vigour that he could find. It echoed down the empty corridor like a thunderclap.

Nickie was still simmering, but at least he had found an outlet, even if it was an inanimate door. When he cooled, he realised that this was Lana's stock in trade, the quick hit to undermine the other person. In the fullness of time he learnt that there were, of course, no actual plans to shut down his subject although budgetary restraint was a cold reality in the light of declining student numbers.

In the coming days, weeks and months Nickie came to know Noah Mertens' ways much better than he had before. He was always shocked by the alacrity with which the nitty-gritty work of the dean was delegated to him in his roles as either acting dean or as associate dean, which was a role that Mertens conferred upon him, strangely a role that drew no allowance for the extra duties. For Mertens it was a role that he sought no approval to confer and which he never spoke to the hierarchy about. He merely had his personal assistant organise a sign for Nickie's door. It was then a certainty that Nickie, not versed in the skills of self-promotion would likely simply do the work without querying why or how.

Moots came and went, and the gradual climb upwards had begun.

Nickie marvelled also at the alacrity of Mertens' annual mid-year disappearance.

"You know," Mertens would say, "they give me a flat in a nice old building in the centre of London. It has high ceilings and is very big. I teach my course there intensively and I can now do this in my sleep. And they pay me well. And I can go to Wimbledon. You like tennis?"

"Er... yes, it's a wonderful event."

"I love tennis and strawberries and Champagne, especially Champagne. And they pay me a lot of money for teaching there. I will never give it up."

On this day in May, Mertens was still in residence at the Besser block university. He summoned Nickie into his office and asked about the moot court bench before he announced his new money-making scheme.

"One of my former mooters, Alexander Amore, is Legal Counsel at Fremantle Shipping Company. One of the problems associated with the executives there is that they cannot give speeches and communicate that well. So, we will use the moot court bench to give them a series of seminars on communication. This is very good for the reputation of the law school."

"Is that really our role?" queried Nickie with an incredulous look on his face. "I thought the moot court bench existed to create training in advocacy for our student body, not to educate outsiders. They are not really equipped to act as trainers in this context and the pressures on them are already great." Nickie paused and he could see a rebuke coming, but, before it manifested, he threw in one last opinion. "Is this really fair on them to expect them to do this."

"This is an ideal job for them to do. It is part of why I established the bench, to serve the interests of the law school. This is what I want. You know no one is irreplaceable." Mertens had spoken and Nickie, who was listening to the message to back off and follow orders, wondered how he could possibly sell this idea to the students on the Moot Court Bench, students who would surely see right through this ego-based project.

The meeting was over quickly and Nickie slumped as he walked back towards his office. The mishandling of the moot court students was not something he wished to promote.

He spoke aloud when he at last sat at his desk in his office.

"Brown paper packages full of money. These are a few of my favourite things."

He was lost in a dark reverie when the telephone on his desk rang.

It was China calling.

Nickie had never been to China. He had been to Singapore once to work at a university 'expo' designed to recruit Singaporean students who had missed out on obtaining a position at the National University of Singapore. Most of his travels had been to the United Kingdom, European countries such as Germany and to the new world, the United States and Canada. He had never thought much about Asia even though it was on his country's doorstep. Now his life was to change irreversibly and forever. The taste of Asia was on his lips, but he never even knew it.

Chapter 11
The Good Dean

This was not the sandstone university. It was, properly speaking, a Besser block university, a concrete jumble, which was designed and constructed in haste to a tight and inflexible budget. The differences between the group of eight universities and the other Australian universities is quite considerable. There are financial resources differences, and there are also visual differences. The sandstone university featured its beautiful and historic sandstone buildings constructed around a quadrangle. It was symmetry personified (if such a thing were possible) and it was also elegant, pleasing, and comforting. This university was basic. Its architecture suggested a utilitarian approach. It existed to do the basics comfortably well, which was fair enough as far as that went. However, there were literally no signs of aspiration, not even the faintest sign no matter how humbly constructed. At six p.m. each night there was no hustle and bustle of university life. It was like a neglected ghost town from the American west, only it was located in the Australian west.

Mertens had left the sandstone university and become dean at the Besser block university. To use

Australian colloquial language now he was 'stoked' to then be promoted to the position of executive dean over both the law school and the business school. Although this university was not the sandstone university, and he briefly grieved for that, he knew that now he could construct his empire anew and even more effectively than at his old university. Now his empire had grown exponentially as he was elevated to a position above most others. He was a success. In this new position he could plan, take on work at other universities, make lots of money teaching elsewhere, because this position freed him up to provide oversight and to manage the chairs on the deck without ever having to take responsibility. In the wake of his promotion, there was a need to find a new dean of law, someone who could be loyal to Mertens but who Mertens could 'influence'.

The man Noah Mertens chose was Tim Andrews. He chose Tim even before the interview because influencing job interviews was Mertens' stock in trade. He was an artist when it came to manipulating membership of the interview panel in order to have it make the decision he had already made.

Mertens knew Tim Andrews to be someone he could work with and someone he felt he could manage. They had known each other for a long time and had worked together to teach the arbitration course to assist those who wished to qualify as arbitrators. Both members of staff had an interest in alternative dispute resolution methods, especially international arbitration and mediation. Both had coached in the Vis Moot, and Andrews was addicted to assisting student mooting involvement. However, while they were colleagues in some activities, and they were always collegial, there were some differences.

At the interview Andrews was asked about his vision for the law school should he be appointed.

"I have a plan," said Tim, "I think we need a very balanced approach to everything. Each academic should teach, research and write and do service to the law school and the university community or the community at large."

"You mean like the Legal Aid Unit?" queried the HR (Human Resources) person, Amanda Stone.

"Well, no," said Andrews thinking that he was walking off a precipice into total oblivion. "I was more thinking of service to the university, by participating in recruiting events and service to the profession by making submissions to the Law Reform Commission and service to the students through involvement in international activities, exchanges, mooting and so on."

"How do you feel about our legal aid service?"

"Well I think it is important to maintain what we have, but, you know, it creates great budgetary pressures and, when all is said and done, it is not a core responsibility of any law school. Generally speaking, the way to go is to lock into existing services. But, of course, as a matter of fact and historical fact, we have our own Legal Aid Centre. I would maintain it but would not support its expansion on both financial and philosophical grounds."

There were some frowns among the interviewing panel at this response, but Mertens did his job to persuade.

"What would you do about the school's research deficit?"

"Well, one of the first things I would do, would be to devise a mentoring scheme. We need to nurture and encourage," said Tim. "Actually, we need to push staff to produce more work. Their productivity is abysmal and that is kind."

The interview was soon enough over and a few days later Tim sat down with Noah Mertens in a coffee shop to have a comfortable, off-the-record, discussion.

"The old guard are a problem," said Noah, "they have been around since the beginning of the law school, and they simply do not have a work ethic. They are used to having everything their way, so they are not productive, and the university gets angry with the law school because it is unproductive, especially with research and writing. The old guard are crap academics. They should not even be here they are so mediocre. They are worse than mediocre. However, they are dangerous because they have tentacles everywhere, tentacles everywhere. You have to be careful."

"One thing you must not do is to make trouble for Lana. She is not really a bad person but, you know, things will get out of hand very quickly and the old guard know how to organise and work together to undermine you. Mark my words. Do not create trouble for Lana or you will regret it."

"I do not really want to make trouble for anyone, but you know with the old guard I feel no one has a divine right to escape work. We all have a certain workload that we all have to perform and to not become immune to well-worn obligations as a productive scholar and academic."

"I hear what you say," Tim continued, "but deep down I feel that everyone should be accountable. Really, even Lana should be accountable and should not seek to be unaccountable."

"Be that as it may, but if you do not listen to me on this, they will turn on you as a group."

'I say to you," said Mertens, "stay away from her or things will get a lot worse."

In the Australian system the vice-chancellor is the key person at the university. They may have a ceremonial chancellor but, in a day to day sense, the vice-chancellor functions much as a chief executive might in the business context, he or she calls the shots and runs the university. Each university has a council or senate for policy and decision-making processes but, in a day-to-day sense, everyone on campus is answerable to the vice-chancellor.

The vice-chancellor at the Besser block university, Professor Rupert Ruggles, was newly installed. Befitting a less confident university, there was no appointment from within and they chose an Englishman from one of those Midlands universities in the United Kingdom. If they came from England, well, they came from the world of Shakespeare, Oxford and Cambridge Universities, places where as a graduate you only have to attend some dinners and they automatically confer a Master's degree on you. Only the UK institutions could get away with such capers and only because of the reality of the cultural cringe existing in the places like Australia and parts of Asia.

The function was glittering. Money had not been spared and waiters hovered around the guests like moths drawn to a light. The function had been called to create a splash associated with the opening of a new research and teaching centre at the Besser block university.

"It is my great pleasure," said Vice-Chancellor Dr Rupert Ruggles, "to announce the establishment of a new research and teaching centre, which represents a brilliant new initiative for study of the big picture issues of public policy in the contemporary world. We have assembled outstanding scholars and academics to research, write, teach and run what will become a profoundly influential and affecting centre at national, regional and global levels. I now call upon my wife Dr Phillis Clarke, who also happens to be the Foundation Director of this centre, to accept this plaque to commemorate the opening of the Australian Centre for Public Policy and International Relations."

Lana always knew her mark and could readily find a way to focus exclusively on the most powerful person in the room.

"Oh, you are from the law school," said Rupert when he was cornered by Lana.

"They need to do a bit more research and writing there but, apart from that, it seems to be a very well-run unit."

"Oh no, no we have some severe problems," said Lana with a serious look on her face. "Problems of leadership!"

"Oh, I am sorry to hear that. Perhaps we should meet for you to tell me more."

"Yes Vice-Chancellor, I would like that very much. Perhaps you can give me a call and we can meet. Here is my card."

"And mine." Rupert handed her his business card.

"We could meet off the campus if that would suit you, and you can tell me more. I am sure my university credit card could cover a lunch somewhere."

Several days later the night was still relatively young as the VC's personal assistant wrapped up her work and bid her boss goodnight. The office was now empty when Rupert reached for his phone.

"Lana, come over now. We can continue our discussions about what is wrong with the law school."

Although the tryst began on his desk in a somewhat traditional, quick sex format, she knew it was only a matter of time before she could take her rightful position on top. She loved being on top. The sex was not satisfactory until she had achieved a complete domination over the hapless male. She loved pulling the levers to enslave not just his body, but also his mind. She was a stealer of souls and of wills.

"You must come to our barbecues," said Lana as she bid the VC goodbye after one of their encounters. She felt liberated and in control of everything that might impact upon her life. She felt empowered as though she ruled the world and all of these pathetic men would leap to obey her word or to face exposure.

Tim Andrews was shocked when he looked closely at his staff's unproductive publications record both in terms of quality and especially deficient in terms of quantity. Tammy Turner was a US citizen, although she had worked and lived in Australia for many years. Her performance review meeting was to prove to be memorable to Tim for many reasons, mostly negative reasons.

"Tammy, you have just returned from sabbatical leave, which I had hoped would lead to some publications. Your scholarly publications are really important to the law school's ranking and the university's ranking. Sabbatical leave is always approved on the basis that it is not a holiday but in order to write articles. I cannot yet see anything coming out of your sabbatical. You must have some articles you are working on."

'Nuh," said Tammy as she rocked back in her chair and placed both of her arms on the back of her head, the classic know-all body language, "nothing. I had a lot time for meditating, for thinking about things, for feeling good vibes and enjoying life."

"Yes, but have you written anything?"

"I wrote a case note for the *Lawyer* magazine."

"Well it is better than nothing, but not much because we cannot count it as it is a professional newsletter not a scholarly journal of standing. It is as good as nothing."

"Well I had a good time on sabbatical."

"Err… yes."

"You don't think the university really cares?" asserted Tammy, and Tim was beginning to wonder if she was right. "They don't care."

"I think they will. Is there no way you can write something from what you have been looking at in a professional sense while you were on leave?"

"No."

"But what did you do during that time?" said Tim.

"I thought about things. I meditated but there was no time for academic writing. Anyway, as I said, the university never does anything. They don't care. Relax, it will be okay. I got a good suntan."

"As a matter of law, they can ask you to repay the cost of your salary in full if you have been unproductive."

"They won't do that. I have friends. I go to barbecues."

Tim wondered, *What have barbecues to do with anything?* "You need to salvage your academic career by writing something soon. You really do."

When Andrews spoke about this interview to the new executive dean, Mertens' advice did not help in Andrew's eyes.

They sat in the coffee shop.

"Ah," said Mertens, "she is a member of the old guard. She is a crap academic, but you know the old guard have friends in the institution. You may not be able to get your own way. I would leave her alone and work around her."

Tim Andrews took a long, hard look at Mertens in that moment, and he saw just another self-serving academic who he felt would probably never put himself on a limb to support his dean. He felt he, Andrews, was walking down a long, lonely alleyway on his own. Mertens was supposed to be covering his back, but he had ducked into a building and was no longer on the scene. Andrews felt alone, very alone. The realisation that possibly no one had his back deeply concerned him. He wondered how hellish his life might eventually become.

One day, a week later, Dean Tim Andrews was walking down a corridor when he came across Francisco Kreuger who was always keen to talk. Kreuger's idea of what it was to talk to someone was a little different to some others. With Francisco 'to talk' was more to engage in one-way conversation than to truly engage with the other person in a meaningful two-way conversation. What obsessed Francisco was his own enterprise, his own needs and desires.

"Ah, Timothy I must tell you about my latest article. It is about freedom of speech in Hong Kong. You might be interested. It is a wonderful article…".

At this point Tim Andrews had already become hypnotised by Francisco, but not in a good way. He fell into a zombie zone knowing he was expected to listen but not participate, other than in praise. At the same time his mind began wandering, as he found his soul lost in a world of meaningless expressions and nods of recognition and understanding, when everything said was flowing through him and down a stream of consciousness somewhere, somewhere else. He knew not where. As this was happening, Lana passed by them both. Tim's back was to her and he did not see, did not know that for a moment she appeared in the corridor and like a ghost as quickly disappeared.

Lana was to be next cab off the rank for the annual performance appraisal conducted by the dean. Tim was ever hopeful but after he looked at her performance appraisal form, he felt otherwise. She declined to complete the form, instead scrawling on it in pen, "None of your business!" Afterwards he wrote an email to her indicating the compulsory nature of the requirement to complete a performance appraisal meeting with the dean, which was met by a terse, "Get stuffed! I answer to no one!" Tim completed the remainder of the form indicating her non-compliance.

Vice-Chancellor Rupert Ruggles lifted his office telephone to his ear and dialled Lana's number.

"My wife is away," he said. "I have booked a hotel for us, presidential suite, on my work credit card. We can have a luxurious weekend together."

He listened quietly to her response.

"Bring your leather. You know how I like your leather," he said.

That night Tim Andrews and his wife Nina were having a quiet dinner at a restaurant in Fremantle. They were sitting at a window and Tim had an unobstructed view of the goings-on in the street outside the restaurant. He and Nina were sipping on the soup they had ordered as entrées. His wife as always, could transact the soup smoothly into her mouth, where Tim always struggled. There was also a certain quotient of his soup that spilled onto the tablecloth during the process of consumption.

When Tim looked up from the table, he could see a group of tartily dressed women cavorting up the street. They were loud and as they came more and more into focus, he noticed some deeper voices among their number and that their figures were either rather slim or falling within the clearly overweight category. Then he noticed one in particular, dressed in a glitzy red evening dress. It looked like someone he knew. For a moment he was mentally in denial but then he commented to his wife.

"Have a look at the group outside Nina. The woman in the red dress looks like Gary Worth. What do you think?"

"Oh, there is a reason," said Nina as she strained her eyes. "That is because it *is* Gary Worth," she said.

Tim returned to the soup with a serious expression on his face. "He didn't put that down as a hobby on his CV."

"He wouldn't, would he?" said Nina.

When Mertens rang Tim Andrews, there was a note of concern in his voice. "HRM want to see both of us right now on a 'serious matter' they said. Do you know what it is about?"

"No, but I will bring some records with me just in case," said Tim. He reached down to his files and he drew out the file for performance appraisal. *Surely it could not be connected with this process. I did the right thing, all by the book,* he thought.

As they walked across the courtyard in the direction of the chancery, what Mertens liked to variously call the Kremlin or the bunker depending upon his mood, they speculated on the urgent meeting.

"This is what they do when they want to fire you," said Mertens.

"Perhaps it is about financial issues," he said as he spoke his thoughts.

"Do you think it may have something to do with the old guard?" asked Tim, half speculating. "You said they were dangerous."

"I hope so." Mertens did not want the focus on his financial practices and his secretion of certain funds in otherwise labelled accounts. He could already in his mind's eye see the security people clearing his desk out. Once you are out, sometimes they make it instantaneous.

When they arrived at the HRM office in the Chancellery they were seated and kept waiting for five minutes. Then they were sat down in a room before Kelly Martin, the Senior Manager in the Human Resources Management office and Sharon McDuff, her assistant.

"What is this all about?" asked Mertens timidly as he wondered which skeleton under his bed they were about to resurrect.

Kelly took the initiative in replying.

"Professor Andrews, we have received several complaints of bullying regarding the performance appraisal interviews. We have also had a specific complaint from a member of staff saying that you refused to say hello to them in the hallway. They saw that as part of your bullying."

One of the complaints is that you wrote comments about the member of staff when you did not even give them an opportunity to participate in the review."

"Are you referring to Lana?" asked Tim.

"We are not at liberty to divulge any names to you. This would compromise the integrity of the process."

"Well, we also need due process and to face our accuser. This is a basic of any legal system in a democratic country. And trust me, I will sue on this one." Tim foraged in his performance appraisal files.

"Look at this!" he said as he offered up the performance appraisal on which Lana had written 'None of your business!'. "You also might like to have a look at this which is her follow-up email. He handed across a printout of the email on which Lana had written, 'Get stuffed! I answer to no one.'

"In point of fact, what we have here is an attempt at upward bullying and we have a demonstrably vexatious complaint based on untruth. This is clear academic misconduct, don't you agree?"

Martin who had been studying both items, looked up. "If the executive dean is prepared to so recommend," she said, "there most definitely is enough here to proceed with a process that will lead to dismissal." Mertens and Tim Andrews were soon on their way back to the law school walking across the main quadrangle of the university.

"If you like I will write up the academic misconduct charge for you," said Tim. "We can finally bring justice about."

"No," said Mertens. "No one tells me what to do. HR here are shit. They cannot tell me what to do. They do not know how to run the law school. They have no idea."

"But this is for us too," said Tim, "she is a millstone around our neck. This is our chance."

"No," repeated Mertens. "I will not do what they want. *I* am in charge, not them."

Tim was shocked beyond belief. He was stunned into silence. Here was the golden chance to rid themselves of this evil person. How could Mertens not act upon the golden opportunity? Tim was frozen with anger, frozen by anxiety, frozen by confusion.

What he did not know was what was going on in Mertens' mind, his memories of the sexual acts he and Lana shared and his fear of exposure to his wife, to everyone, his fear of Lana herself, her anger, her wrath, her revenge. His mind was a cesspool of fear and self-interest.

That day Dean Tim Andrews left work early. He drove to the outskirts of Perth and parked his car where he could look at two signs. One led back to the city. The other was for the Great Western Highway that led out of Perth and, eventually, across the Nullarbor Plain, the longest straightest highway in the world. It led across the desert to the eastern states. There were tears running out of his eyes as he sat there contemplating his life, so successful, so undermined. He felt and looked shattered. Although the tears were running down his face he was not sobbing. They were entirely spontaneous, just the emotion pouring out from within him. He sat there quietly, contemplating until dark came, when he elected to turn his car back towards the city and his home, his wife, his child, his bastion against the cruel world... until next time.

When he returned to work, he had an unexpected visit from Sharon McDuff the assistant to the HRM manager.

'I just called to see how you were doing, and to collect the academic misconduct documentation if it is available yet," she said.

Tim clenched his hands and there was a long pause before he answered.

"There is not going to be an accusation of academic misconduct."

"Oh."

"Mertens refuses to act against her. I just don't understand."

"What you need to understand, is that none of this is your fault. It relates to matters that others should have addressed in the past and failed to do so. He should have addressed these issues when he first came in as dean. That was his opportunity. Instead, it suited him to do nothing. And he is still doing nothing. Some of us see how she operates, how he operates. The thing is it is not your fault. Don't beat up on yourself. It is the failure of those above you and it has gone on for years."

Tim thought that this was to be his worst time as dean. He was wrong.

The very evening that Mertens declined to support Tim Andrews, Lana was attending to the Vice-chancellor, eminent Professor Rupert Ruggles, in an executive hotel room in Sydney. His immediate lustful needs were being met, and she was paying a deposit that would ensure that her will prevailed in the law school now and into the future. This was even better than the copious amounts of pornography he was downloading on his work computer. Lana could not read his thoughts beyond the immediate physical acts he desired to complete with her. She was more concerned with her own requirements as she was in process of becoming the queen of his mind and the queen of the university.

The email came from Human Resources Management. It was from the Director of HRM at the Besser block university informing him of a decision that was made by the vice-chancellor. Tim was speechless. He read the words over and over again. No, he was not hallucinating. He thought *I have won moots, I have won national teaching awards, research awards and yet now, now my contract is not being renewed.*

When he sat in Noah Mertens' office he felt like he was the one who was being inundated. Surely there were things going on behind the scene. Who was betraying him, who was running interference, who was influencing the vice-chancellor against him? He did not know but he was beginning to feel squeamish and uncomfortable around anyone he had trusted or confided in, no matter how small or trivial the confidence.

"Did you have any knowledge of this?" he asked Mertens.

"Me, no, definitely not!" asserted Mertens with mock indignation as if he was saying to Andrews, 'How could you be so disloyal as to suggest this of me. I am shocked and disappointed in you.'

"You may need to be more careful about who you speak to," pronounced Mertens.

"I confide in no one person," said Tim earnestly. "I only tell my wife a little, because I do not want to upset her. Apart from you, there is almost no one else I would consider confiding in. My personal assistant, who I brought with me from the other university has access, but she is not one of the old guard, so I trust her."

"You know the old guard invite her to their barbecues," pronounced Mertens. "You need to be sure you can trust her. If they turn her, they have access to every decision you make."

There was a long silence as Tim reflected. *How could Mertens know about the attendance at barbecues unless he had also been in attendance?* Tim's mind was whirring with possible associations and betrayals.

"With my record I get this. You know that I won teaching excellence awards, research awards, international mooting competitions. In my areas of specialisation, I am seen as a leader by the industry. I just do not understand how they can arrive at this decision. How can it possibly be justified?"

"I told you before, the old guard have connections. You are so naïve Tim."

Tim had repressed his anger forever and you cannot do that, and expect for pressure not to build up. His volcano was ready to explode and his blood was up. He was an Aries and he did not take prisoners at such times. His placid demeanour gave way to uncompromising assertion. "I'd rather be naïve than corrupt," he said. And he didn't care at this moment about the consequences for having queried the motivation of 'he who should only be adored and praised.'

"What do you mean?" Mertens was flush with anger and nearly leapt to his feet. "You must not be talking about me!"

"If the cap fits, wear it! You had your opportunity to support me, and you refused to act."

"I will not be dictated to by HRM. I act when I want to act."

"Exactly. Whatever she has on you it must be good. I hope you enjoyed it, because you are paying a big price. Makes me wonder who really runs the law school, her or you?"

Their conversation ended abruptly as Tim walked from the room, and slammed the door behind him. He could just hear Mertens calling out after him. "I am loyal to my wife." Deep down they both knew this was a blatant lie.

Later that day he broke the news to Francisco when they met in the coffee shop. As usual they had to go through a charade that would lead to Tim paying the bill for the coffees. This time it was a pretty basic strategy adopted, an oldie but a good one.

"Oh, I just need to go to the rest room," said Francisco.

"What kind of coffee do you want?" asked Tim directly. "I will order them while you are away."

"Oh, cappuccino please."

"I've got it."

When Francisco returned, and Tim unburdened himself of the events that saw him now consider Mertens as a betrayer. "Surely," said Tim Andrews, "Noah would not have actually gone to a barbecue with the old guard. That is how they recruit and influence people to their cause. Hardly a just cause."

"Oh yes," said Francisco, "I know for a fact he has attended at least one of those meetings. I was not so sure he wanted to be there. You know he always criticises the 'old guard'. He sees them as lazy and weak and incompetent."

"But if he fraternises with them," asserted Andrews, "we are judged by the people we associate with, whether we like it or not."

"He and Lana are strange bedfellows. And you know he says he loves only his wife. He is very aggressive about that."

"Perhaps he doth protest too much. Perhaps they are strange bedfellows." Tim paused to reflect and then continued. "It would explain a lot. It would explain how and why he is so reluctant to act against her."

"It would explain why he is so reluctant to act against her if they have a relationship."

"Have I told you about my latest book? It is about the constitutions of South America. I have a foreword by the Chief Justice of the High Court. It is my proudest work and there will be a big release in Sydney next month. You should come."

"Thank you, but no," said Tim. "You must remember that my contract will not be renewed. I am in the process of walking out the door."

Tim soon was lost again in his contemplation of all the evil networks that might be operating near and around the law school. While he knew Mertens' comment about Tim being naive was a put down, he also knew that Mertens himself was surely anything but naive.

His last memory of Mertens that night, when he lay in his bed to go to sleep, was of Noah Mertens taking his watch off and waving it in Tim's face. "I have had this for twenty-five years and it only cost me $5 — twenty-five years!" The memory of a man who was unwilling to pay the price of holding true to friendship, or of even returning loyalty, haunted him from that night forward to long after he had driven out of the gates of the university after his forced retirement.

Chapter 12
Episode 5: Time, what has become of you?

The university was sited in a suburb on the south side of Perth, Western Australia, being a state of Australia, located on its west coast. Perth is the most isolated capital city in the world. To its east lies the Nullarbor Plain. To its west is the Indian Ocean and to its south the Great Southern Ocean. Perth is the most beautiful new city in Australia. Its skies seem a continued presence, so vast, so beautiful and changeable, like the moods of a princess. There is always a presence above you of a vast and beautiful environment, a beauty beyond mere words.

The university itself was a shabby presence. It was not exactly a sandstone, group of eight university like the Ivy League Universities of the United States. The sad truth was that it was a cut-price university trying to compete with the sandstone university. It could still achieve moments of greatness, but they were fleeting and far between, and it was looked down upon by the establishment for its physical appearance. It was a Besser block university not a sandstone university. Nevertheless, it marketed itself actively, claiming unique experiences and to aspire to excellence. It was like a Jack Russell nipping at the heels of an elephant, the occasionally moribund but historic and establishment-supported sandstone universities.

In the moot room of the Besser block university a team is preparing before Nickie Jones to compete in the 2008 Space Law Moot.

Inside the Moot Court Room, a white female mooter stands at the lectern mooting to the 2008 Space Law Mooting Competition problem in practice before Nickie, her coach, and team members.

"Your Excellencies, the appellant submits that the Republic of Usurpia's decision to authorise the relocation of the Satelsat-18 satellite in the face of Concordia's objections is contrary to international law."

"Your Excellencies, first I will submit that Usurpia breached Article VIII of the Outer Space Treaty by authorising Satelsat-18's relocation. Your Excellencies, I have three arguments in support of this submission. Your Excellencies, first it was Concordia who actually possessed jurisdiction and control over Satelsat-18 satellite because it, Concordia, and not Usurpia was the state of registry. Your Excellencies, second, I will argue that Concordia retained jurisdiction and control over Satelsat-18, because these rights were not transferred. Your Excellencies, my third argument is that Usurpia interfered with Concordia's jurisdiction and control, by actually authorising the relocation of Satelsat-18. Your Excellencies, I move now to my first argument."

The wall clock accelerates through fourteen minutes of submissions before the mooter concludes.

"Your Excellencies, this concludes the submissions of the applicant states, Landia and Concordia. Your Excellencies; that is unless there are any further questions that Your Excellencies care to ask me."

Nickie sits on the bench as a judge, in simulation of the proceedings of the International Court of Justice. Despite the cerebral intensity of the activity, there is just a slight sense of mischief in his eyes as he speaks.

"Well indeed you are mooting before the International Court of Justice, and, as the judge, I should be referred to as Your Excellency. But (searches for words) you have used the word over a hundred times in fourteen minutes of legal argument literally at the beginning of every sentence. *Every sentence.* You need to vary your sentences and begin with something else. At present you are using "Your Excellency" as a crutch to prop up your sentences and you overdo the respect. Such a thing is possible. You numb the effect of the word through overuse. It has the opposite effect to what you intend. Yes, there is no sincerity like feigned sincerity. Don't take away from the respect you are trying to show, just not so many 'your excellencies' eh?"

Chapter 13
Margaret River — Years Later

Margaret River township is located south of Perth in Western Australia. It is an easy two and a half to three hours' drive south of Perth to reach arguably Australia's most exquisitely beautiful wine region.

Nickie, now with a walking stick, limping and older, was out walking his pet greyhound. They turned onto the main shopping area of the township, which was a strip shopping centre with coffee shops, an old hotel, boutique shops and a petrol station half way down with the obligatory supermarket hidden just down an alleyway.

It was now winter and the wild weather was not far away. The sky that towers majestically above everything in Western Australia was now laden with swirling and dramatic clouds. It was grey and menacing.

Nickie took a seat at a sidewalk table of a coffee shop and the dog curled up at his feet. A waitress, in her early thirties and out of shape, placed his coffee on the table.

"Thanks."

Nickie tapped the table with two fingers from his right hand in the bent, serving gesture to say thank you, as done in China and Hong Kong, without thinking. The lady serving the coffee reacted with a slight frown.

Nickie looked up at the overcast sky.

"Doesn't look so good."

"Yeah," said the coffee shop worker, "no tennis today."

Stating what had been on his mind Nickie responded.

"My girl used to play tennis."

Memories of the Hong Kong connection flood into his mind. Memories of his lost love, which were ever-present in his head despite rejection and the passage of time, and the world moving on all around him.

"And badminton," he added.

The waitress nodded and walked off, indifferent.

Nickie looked down at the dog. Talking now to the dog and to thin air.

"Badminton was a big deal in Hong Kong."

The weather closed in rapidly. The sky was turbulent, wild and wilful. Suddenly a mantle of grey mist fell over the township. A few spits, and then the rain began to beat down. The wind blew the rain into horizontal mode. In an instant, anyone out in the open and unprotected, became saturated.

As the outside tables were rapidly cleared, the barista appeared and seeing Nickie still seated there with a partly drunk cup of coffee in front of him called out, "Bring the dog inside. Otherwise you'll both freeze to death and drown."

Nickie rose from his table as the dog began a preliminary shake.

"Lots of things to die from eh Spider?"

Inside the coffee shop things were much cosier. There was more heat, and despite the café blinds that kept out the rain wobbling a little, it was dry and protected from the rain. A good thing on such a day.

A short time later the place was empty, save Nickie and Spider. The barista sauntered over and sat opposite Nickie. After the obligatory references to the changeable weather, their conversation was well underway.

"A professor! At a Hong Kong university. That's a long way from Margaret River." He paused as he reflected.

"How'd you end up there?"

After ruminating for a long moment, Nickie said, "Everything led me there. My interest in space law. The marriage break-up. It was exotic China, and they asked me nicely. It was because of mooting."

"What in God's name is mooting?" exclaimed the barista.

Feeling that he was trying to shrink his world into a simple explanation, Nickie felt he could not condense his world thus, but knew he had to give some explanation.

"It's when law students dress up in suits and argue a legal case in front of judges. Two teams compete. One represents the applicant state and the other the opposition, the respondent state. It simulates proceedings before the International Court of Justice. It also value-adds the students and, if they succeed at international level, they get offers from the law firms."

The barista seemed to get the gist of it. "So it's like an international game in football."

Nickie nodded. It wasn't a bad analogy. "I suppose so ... the legal equivalent."

A look of doubt passed across the face of the barista. "Err... you said space law. What's space law? Is there really such a thing?"

Nickie had heard this dirge so many times before and sighed. But he resolved not to show his frustration.

"You have a mobile phone, yes? (the barista nodded quizzically.) Well, the contracts between you and your provider are not the only ones in play. There are also the contracts between your provider and the satellite operator. There is a launch of that communications satellite, so things can go wrong there or in orbit. Satellites fail, and sometimes they even collide or cause debris. Same applies to TV. No satellites in space, no international TV. And, of course, the leading spacefaring states want to get their greedy, grubby little hands onto all the mineral wealth on the celestial bodies like the moon and Mars, helium-3 and titanium, the mineral riches."

The barista seemed to comprehend at least some of what Nickie said. He got it only just that his mobile telephone and the TV signals needed satellites. For an instant he pondered the new perspective and his response was ponderously slow.

"Okay."

Tired of explaining but knowing there was a need to explain further his mind returned to Sydney in 2007.

Chapter 14
To Moot and to Lose

He remembered the New South Wales Supreme Court in Macquarie Street, Sydney, as an imposing building.

He recalled how the judge's eyes followed the mooters attentively. He remembered his mooter Shane, standing before a bench composed of three eminent commentators, two older men and a younger Canadian woman.

Shane spoke excitedly as he launched his critical rebuttal point. The moot could potentially be won or lost on the one point. The excitement got the better of Shane who had never stuttered before this moment, the critical moment of the final.

"Your Ex- excellencies, the a-a-agent f-f-for the… the state er state o-o-o-of Utopia has n-n-not se-se-told… is not accurate in say saying the — the that there is an exclusion zone of 500 kilometres al-al-al allowable u-u-u-under the Chicago Con- con convention. But, but it .. it only allows fe-fe-fi-five hundred m-m-metres."

In the audience, Nickie leaned across and whispered into the ear of the third member of the team, Julie, a Chinese Australian woman.

"Five hundred metres not five hundred kilometres. She lied, but he stuffed up his words. They won't believe him even though it is the truth, unless they check which they won't. That would be too much to expect."

"This," said Shane, "concludes our surrebuttal."

Shane closed his presentation folder and gathered together a few loose sheets of paper, and was about to leave the lectern, when the Canadian judge leaned forward and addressed him.

"One last question. You mentioned the *S.S. Lotus* case. What was the name of the ship involved? Can you recall?"

Unflinchingly, Shane replied.

"The *Boz-Kourt*, your Your Excellency."

"Thank you, counsel." She smiled and that smile embedded hope in Nickie's heart, a hope that her views might be decisive. To know the name of the ship, required a certain cognitive disposition for in-depth research.

The President of the Court was more impassive.

"Well, that concludes proceedings now. We retire to decide on the winner, and we will see many of you this evening at the dinner, where the result will be announced."

The teams shook hands and the members of the audience drained from the courtroom. Nickie found himself in the imposing foyer (yes even the foyers of such buildings can justly be referred to as being 'imposing") where the coach or minder of a Chinese team approached him.

"Dr Jones, I am Charles He from Kai Tak University in Hong Kong, congratulations. Your team makes the final. I have a team here, Mike and Carmen, but they do not have experience. We always do badly. Can you help us next time? We need guidance."

Nickie responded immediately, but the cogs in his brain were whirring. At that time, the Chinese teams had yet to win the moot. He knew there were some good teams and some great universities there, but so far, the moot had been dominated by the National University of Singapore and the Australian and New Zealand teams. He wanted to assist the Chinese based teams to be more than competitive.

"Nice to meet you Charles. Yes," he said, "we need to elevate the Chinese teams. The Chinese kids are as bright, if not brighter, than the western kids. They just need the right training. Perhaps we can have a practice moot next time around. I had one recently with a Beijing-based university."

Nickie remembered the Beijing-based team and the moot court screens on which their images were projected via the internet connection. He remembered particularly the mooter from China who stood before him, as judge, making her submissions.

"The obligation to return astronauts is unconditional obligation according to Professor Bin Cheng."

"So what did Bin Cheng literally say?" queried Nickie. "Can you assist the court on that?"

Silence prevailed. "Do you have a quote?"

The mooter fumbled amongst the hellishly disorganised pile of loose papers on the lectern in front of her. A long period of shuffling followed, as she predictably struggled to find anything on what the eminent commentator had said.

"Er, mmm, yes, yes. I er... mmm cannot assist."

Her head dropped in defeat, and then she looked up with a pleading look in her eyes.

Nickie smiled as he looked at her with a kindly, but resolute look on his face.

"Just say 'Your Excellency, I am unable to assist you on this point', and move on or better still find the quote from Bin Cheng. It should not be hard. He is the leading commentator. And then when you offer it up I go 'Wow, she is well prepared, well resourced. She is offering up something not just bluffing her way through.' It makes a difference. If you have an alternative submission you can also, after restating your position, go, in any event 'Your Excellency, our case does not hinge on this point alone. I will now move our alternative submission which is... etcetera, etcetera, etcetera...'"

"Oh," said the mooter with the look of a lost sheep on her face.

It was April 2007 and the awards night of the Asia-Pacific Zone of the Space Law Moot. The awards were presented at a restaurant in a sandstone building at the Rocks, Sydney. The Rocks is one of Sydney's oldest areas and is in the shadows of the harbour bridge. It is also within easy walking distance of Circular Quay and the Sydney Opera House precinct.

Mickey Liu, the Asia-Pacific coordinator of the moot, an Australian citizen of Chinese descent, and Hong Kong born, paused before he announced the winner of the competition.

The two teams that were finalists sat at the same table. Both were Australian teams, the last time Australian teams were to dominate the event. Nickie's team was one of those teams. Shane and Julie sat next to Nickie. Teams always feel just a little nervous at such times as the wait for the final words of the competition.

"The winner of the Asia-Pacific round of the International Space Law Mooting Competition in 2007 is... the University of..."

Nickie switched off as soon as he heard "University of" because that was not his team. He was stoic in defeat, tried to be gracious in defeat but it was a hard pill to swallow. The other team erupted with joy, and he and his team rose to shake their hands. They then sat down and a moment later their eyes met in collective disappointment. As the other team accepted the winning trophy, Nickie muttered to himself.

"Truth the casualty."

In Margaret River, the rain still tumbled down on that wild and windswept day. It was now a day of memories for Nickie.

With a look of slight discontent on his face the barista spoke.

"Your story. Tell me your story."

"Err… yes," said Nickie, "I am easily deflected. The habits of a life of service to a 24/7 profession."

The barista was now fiddling behind the counter and his head popped up momentarily, "You said," he said, "that you had a divorce."

"Yes," said Nickie soberly.

The barista was still fiddling with equipment and pots and pans beneath the counter. His disembodied voice asked the predictable question.

"So spare me the detail. Give me the highlights."

Nickie sighed like a politician war weary from being asked the same question. "Or low lights. I'll try." He paused.

"You know, I was a boring academic who put his students and his work first. My wife liked to buy stuff. I thought she liked the stuff, her material stuff, more than me."

Nickie's memories were triggered. He recalled, in particular, an evening in his house. He was relaxing, as academics sometimes do, watching television. He had no emotional or physical energy left to do much else. His wife bounced brazenly into the room dressed in gym gear and holding the keys to her car.

"I'm going to the gym," she announced with a touch of 'I spit in your face' in her tone.

Mesmerised, Nickie reacted with question marks in his voice. "At this hour?"

His wife continued towards the door and out the door.

"Expect me when you see me."

Now alone, Nickie exclaimed, "You've got to be joking!"

Next, Nickie's mind leapt to being in his room at the Besser block university. There was a knock on the door. Nickie moved to and opened the door, which revealed two police officers holding a document and looking very serious. He was about to be served with a DVO, a Domestic Violence Order.

The police officer advanced the papers he was holding towards Nickie.

"Are you Nicholas Jones?" he asked. Nickie nodded in assent. "This is a domestic violence order. It tells you that you have been excluded from the family home. You are not allowed to go within a hundred metres of the house. You cannot see or telephone your wife or approach her."

"What? Is this a joke? For *me*?" Nickie responded in mind-blown amazement.

"Yes. There is no mistake. This order is intended for you, and it is legally binding and enforceable. If you breach this order you will be incarcerated. Please read and observe and take this very seriously. Do not attempt to have contact with your wife. Good day."

Many days after this event were now a blur. They say you repress unpleasant memories. Such was the case with Nickie. But he could not repress all memories.

He remembered a new day dawning in a lonely carpark by Coogee Beach, just south of Fremantle in Western Australia.

Nickie had slept all night in the car, hoping that he would not be mugged. He looked and felt rough and sad that he was, however temporarily, without a roof over his head. He left the car and walked out onto the beach and surveyed the dawn from the water's edge. He contemplated a few solitary fishermen, Korean and Chinese, who were fishing resolutely from this pier at Coogee Beach in Perth, Western Australia. A pelican sat stoically on the pole of the light on the pier. Seagulls began to rouse and squawk at each other, and fly out above the water dipping occasionally to swoop in upon their breakfast. A couple of dolphins broke the relatively quiet surface of the water. He watched them move smoothly through the ocean.

Nickie remembered the conversation that drove the truth into his psyche, like a tradesman drives nails into a wooden beam. He felt at these moments like the wooden beam, violated in a sudden and brutal way.

The two of them, Nickie and his work colleague, were having a cup of coffee in a university coffee shop. The colleague spoke.

"When they go to the gym this means they have someone else or are looking for cheap sex. I thought everyone knew that. Gyms are pick-up places."

Nickie reacted flatly, unemotionally. He was still stunned by the finality of the events surrounding him. He felt like an innocent abroad.

"I haven't been near a gym for years. Not my thing."

Nickie's colleague was on a roll. "When they go to a divorce lawyer, the lawyer has a checklist. Number one question is 'Has he hit you?'. When they fail to respond or look like they are going to say 'no' the lawyer adds, 'If he has, it makes it easier to get him out of the house.' Would you like us to take out a DVO order for you? Gentle soul that you are, you never made it beyond question one. Buddy, you never stood a chance."

"I wondered," responded Nickie, "why I never liked family law."

The reply was predictable. "You are," said the colleague, "such an innocent."

"She's supposed to be a Christian."

"Yeah," said the colleague, "with a Teflon god no doubt, made in her own image. A god that always agrees with what she wants."

It was a day like all other term days. Nickie sat at his desk poring over the PowerPoint presentation for his next lecture. He was lost in concentration, when the telephone on his desk rang.

"Hello, Dr Jones," said the voice on the phone, "this is Charles He. I was with the Kai Tak team at the Space Law Moot in Sydney. We spoke."

"Yes, I remember," said Nickie. "Nice to hear from you Charles. What can I do for you?"

"I have Dean Tang here. He wants to talk to you. I will put the phone on hands free."

"We have a big task here. Big job. We want to win moots. Charles says you are expert. We want you to work with our students and to win big honours. Can you come?"

Nickie's mind raced. He knew that he could help them with their programme, but Dean Tang was painting with a broad brush, like many deans do, and there was no detail to consider. He wasn't sure how he should react. It was coming quickly.

"Well, err," bumbled Nickie, "at what level do you propose and on what basis? I mean just for a short visit or contract, fixed term or more permanently?"

In the hours that followed, there was a meeting in Hong Kong within the Law School at Kai Tak University in the dean's office. Those present were Tony D'Silva, the Sri Lankan born deputy dean, a cavernous looking Chinese guy, well-built and tall, Cheng (yes-man type), a chubby Indian academic, more junior but very pally with the dean, one Ramesh Shastri, and the law school's Chief Administration Officer, Ellen Sun.

"Is Tim coming?" asked Ellen. "He is Director of Mooting. Do you want me to call him?"

Tang frowned in response, then, in a peremptory way, stated, "I did not invite Tim. I want to get rid of him. He is typical English, thinks he is the ruler, but he is not. We all know I am the ruler."

At this there were nods and grunts all around the assembled few.

Tony D'Silva could not restrain himself.

"You know what they say, failed in London, then Hong Kong, FILTH."

"I want this Australian, Nickie, to do some coaching for us. Fixed-term contract. Very successful moot coach but, if no results, it is easy for us to get rid of him. I want my friend and colleague Ramesh to be director of moot. If Nickie succeeds I promote Ramesh. If he fails, goodbye Nickie. All good."

"Will this Nickie be a problem for us down the track?" queried Tony. "Will he want to stay? Can we nail him down to one level?"

"Leave that to me," Tang rejoined. "He is our slave, my slave, Ramesh's slave. We will keep him under control and busy. Give Ramesh some slaves and we can make him a big success. We all need slaves. I have many slaves, many, *many* slaves. I placed Ramesh now on my promotions list, not university's list, my list, real list."

At this, there was collective nodding, and all were thinking, *ah yes, the promotions list.* Cheng, who had been quiet, decided to make his contribution to the discussion. "Westerners, they are all hitchhikers. They stay with us a little while and they move on. They are not here for long enough to worry anyone."

For a fleeting moment, Tang's expression became serious. "I want to be the leading law school for moot in China, best in China," he said. "If Doctor Nickie does not give this to us, we throw him out and find someone else."

Nickie could remember the approach to Hong Kong Airport. It had been a red-eye special leaving around midnight. It was early morning in Hong Kong. The sky was typically grey from the pollution spewing across from the entrance to the Pearl River Delta. But as the plane moved below the clouds, he could make out a small island and a myriad of sea vessels, fishing boats and cargo boats below. This was not the approach to the legendary Kai Tak Airport, but the new airport built in the last days of the Brits in Hong Kong before the hand-back to the People's Republic of China, the PRC.

Nickie walked down the jet bridge, then down the big escalator, to an internal train to reach the main terminal, lined up at customs for a brief examination, before buying a ticket and boarding the airport train.

The train flew along its rails beside waterways, wooded, mountainous areas and places that were once fishing villages. They were on the left. He could see communities across the water, bridges being built and soon the apartment block and skyscrapers began to appear. There was Tsing Yi Station and then the port areas, replete with portainers that looked like giant transformers. He listened to Yanni's music on his earphones as he travelled, *Aria* and *Touch of Truth*. They seemed strangely appropriate to his voyage from one culture into another.

They had him visit Hong Kong first as a kind of try-out, to see if he could teach, if he could communicate, if he was made of the right stuff in a manner of speaking. Nickie was bemused by this but he went along with it anyway.

They gave him a PLT or professional legal training class, with the objective being to teach them a little more about advocacy and how judges perceive advocates.

The class consisted of graduate students, seeking to qualify to practise in Hong Kong. The faces in the audience were predominantly Chinese faces with a sprinkling of European ones. This was typical of the East meets West nature of Hong Kong. There were screens in front of the speaker and behind the speaker for the students to take in his PowerPoint slides. The PowerPoint slides that follow appeared when Nickie spoke to the group.

Nickie was introduced to the class by Suraj, who was an academic of Indian ethnicity. Suraj was middle-aged, good looking and elegantly dressed in professional attire, that is, suit and tie. He worked on the Island, that is, Hong Kong Island and taught part-time.

Nickie opened to the following slide:

"*Advocacy Course — Lecture 3*
1. *From the judge's point of view*
2. *Submissions structure.*"

"So, in opening, what is a judge expecting from an advocate?" said Nickie.

"Let's start with a case theory," he continued. "This is your way of opening, to capture what the case is all about from your client's point of view, how they have been wronged. You seek to capture and characterise in a negative sense what the other side has been up to."

"Here is one example, in essence an attempt to capture what the case is all about from your client's point of view, how your client has been wronged."

"Your Honour, we stand before you today because the respondent had a less experienced doctor perform a dangerous operation which he did negligently, and which ruined the life of my client."

Slide 1.

"*Then I expect after that your roadmap, an outline of your submissions, e.g.,*

"*The appellant presents four main submissions. These are, first, that Dr Dare owed my client, Ms Le Nez, a duty of care that involved him performing the operation himself, second, that Dr Dare breach this duty of care, third, that this breach caused the damage and fourth, that the damage, loss of a chance of a lucrative contract, is compensable.*"

Slide 2.

"I will move now to my first submission.

The judge does not want lengthy submissions. The judge wants the core arguments, and the strongest arguments that you have to present.

Prioritise your arguments and, where possible, stick to your plan. If you are taken away from your plan by questioning, make sure that you present your strongest arguments, even if time makes it necessary to delete some points."

Slide 3.

"Questioning from the bench — peeling back the layers of research.

Never cite a case unless you know about it —

- *The facts*
- *Level of court*
- *Judges who sat on bench*
- *Was it a majority decision?*
- *For what proposition does the case stand?*
- *Possible quote from case in support of your arguments — quote page or paragraph number."*

Slide 4.

"Questioning from the bench – peeling back the layers of research

If you make a legal argument or an assertion, and the judge queries it or asks a question, always have support."

Support from where?
the facts of the case

- *the facts of the case*

- *a provision from legislation — statutory interpretation*
- *decisions of other courts — decided cases that may be analogous*
- *the views of a legal commentator where appropriate*
- *a policy reason for so arguing."*

Later on, Nickie could not remember his exact words, except for his ending. He turned to Suraj, who had been sitting in a chair by the door.

"Have I passed the audition?" he asked.

Suraj answered him.

"I suppose they'll tell you when you get back to Australia. I think you did."

Before long Nickie traversed the route back to the airport, had flown back and was once again back at the Besser block university facing his colleague over a cup of coffee.

"Well, have you got the job?" he asked.

"Mmm, yes," said Nickie.

"Well, are you going to take it?"

"Yes, nothing keeping me here," said Nickie. "In fact, everything says go. The dean seems…well… okay."

In Hong Kong, in the multimedia centre, Dean Tang addressed a scholarly conference on mediation. He spoke in his unique way, typically overconfident, unprepared and also, he was marinated in a mixture of Maotai and Australian red wine.

"I am very happy. They tell me that mediation is a trend in trade law, and with my limited knowledge, I believe them. It is a trend in today's world, and we look forward to the future. We may collaborate and work together. You are a friend and you are always welcome at this very law school. Please come to see us if you are passing through. We will always help you. Well, we may not help you, but we will always tell you why. If I am not available, there will always be someone to see you. I do not know who, but someone. Ramesh you can help them."

Back in the coffee shop at Margaret River, Nickie paused to pat his dog. He gave it some of the biscuit that sat by his cup of coffee, which it disposed of in one glorious bite and a little munching.

"To be honest," said Nickie, "I was scared about Hong Kong but more scared by what I had at home. My marriage was over, and I faced the legal firestorm. Blame and vexatious allegations flowed like wine at a wedding. In the end I was desolate, depressed and alone. I wanted to escape but wondered if I had jumped out of the frying pan into the fire, by accepting the position in Hong Kong."

Nickie soon found himself on yet another plane en route to Hong Kong. Once again, he walked down a jet bridge, the bridge between his past and his future, and along the corridors leading through to immigration.

Nickie took one of the red coloured Toyotas that comprise the taxi fleet travelling in the direction of Kowloon Tong, Tsim Sha Tsui (TST) and Hong Kong Island.

As the taxi travelled towards the Kai Tak University it travelled across an extraordinary urban terrain. As it traversed bridges, below there was an extraordinary number of ships in seemingly frenetic activity. The waterfront was studded with huge portainers, standing there like giant transformers ready to clunk into the sea or struggle across the urban landscape, wreaking havoc along the way. The sky was a dull grey, an eerie ghostly presence that suggested a place subject to poor air with pollution aplenty. As the taxi travelled closer towards the city the landscape revealed shabby apartment blocks, where washing hung on poles stuck out of windows, alongside more upmarket newer apartment blocks and a skyline replete with wall-to-wall skyscrapers. However, the cars on the road suggested nothing but luxury, Mercedes, BMWs, Audis, Porches and Ferraris. Under the overpasses a few poor persons clustered, gathering cardboard.

At the law school at Kai Tak University, he soon found himself in the room of the Director of Mooting, Tim Piggott. Tim had first come to Hong Kong from England to serve as a magistrate. From there he had gravitated to the academic life. He was a larger than life Brit. But his overbearing manner reminded Nickie of another era, as if this man was somehow displaced from the British Raj in India. He had just too much condescension, too much arrogance and certainty in his own correctness.

"These kids are primitive," said Piggott, with a conviction that took Nickie by surprise. "They don't speak good English. They don't work hard, and Tang will get rid of you as soon as you fail, and you *will* fail. This is mission impossible working with these students. They have heavy accents and they're not very bright."

Piggott paused to gauge impact then he continued. "They will get rid of you like that." He clicked his fingers demonstratively. "You won't know what has hit you. Don't expect to stay."

Gauging how the field of play lay for Piggott, Nickie calmly replied. "Oh. So far, the kids seem really nice. Unlike the Aussie kids, they do not seem to have a sense of entitlement."

"Your tune will change," insisted Piggott.

Wistfully and gently Nickie responded, "I hope not."

The first night, finding his way back to his apartment using public transport and then taxi, was a challenge for Nickie. The public transport was simple enough to transact. The law school had given him a key ring that he could swipe to travel on the train, and he had worked out how to charge it up with money, so he was pleased with the train trip. Yes, a crowd surged into the train and people pushed hard to be first to any empty seats. And when he went to exit the train there was such a crush of people to get in first, that they seemed to push backwards those who were attempting to exit the train. He wondered if this was only a Kowloon side phenomenon, and whether similar behaviour occurred on the Hong Kong Island lines.

At Hung Hom station, he emerged from the station and both looked and felt confused. He walked past an area roped off by a Falun Gong occupation, and moved to the taxi rank. At the taxi rank he entered a taxi. Unfortunately for Nickie, the driver spoke no English, only Cantonese. This was his first education on how to treat Cantonese-speaking taxi drivers.

"Where do you want to go? (你想去邊道?)" enquired the taxi driver.

Nickie struggled to remember his apartment's name.

"Harbourview Apartments please," said Nickie.

The driver, seemingly puzzled, enquired 'where' in Cantonese.

Nickie foraged in his bag and found a picture of his destination in a brochure in English. He pointed. "There," said Nickie.

The driver responded in Cantonese.

"One street from the water. (海邊隔一個街口)," he grunted. Then feeling a little angry at the neglectful foreigner, he added in Cantonese,

"You are pretty dumb. You don't even know where you live. Dumb foreigner, (你都幾蠢架喎，你連自己住係邊都唔知。白癡鬼佬)"

The driver drove around Hung Hom streets, until he arrived at Harbourview Horizon, one street from Harbourfront Horizon. The driver stopped his taxi there, but Nickie realised it was the wrong place.

"No not the right place," pointing again at the image in the poster.

The driver responded in Cantonese. "Here. This is it. Not it? Where the hell do you want me to go? Try again. Where?"

With steam starting to rise from his head, the driver continued to drive more and more erratically around the streets of Hung Hom, unable to locate the apartments Nickie sought. He eventually stopped back at the train station and charged Nickie. Rather than persisting, Nickie paid and got off back at the train station — from where he started.

After Nickie had paid, the driver, in Cantonese, offered his final words out of the side of his mouth.

"You are a dumb man. Why do we want you here?"

Nickie then took an escalator up one level, and crossed the walkway for the Harbourview Metropolis. He felt unsure, but persisted and walked through the Metropolis and down the escalator, across the freeway at the pedestrian lights and onto a walkway that took him to the entrance of Harbourfront Horizon. Eventually he found his apartment, and entered its foyer feeling tired and with zero emotional energy left. He had learned the lesson of where he lived in relation to the train station and the university.

The next morning, Nickie looked out on Victoria Harbour with a cup of coffee in his hand. The enterprise there was amazing. Cruise ships, ferries and older vessels like junks, all plied their troth on the harbour. The sky was typically grey, but the skyscrapers on the other side, on the Hong Kong side, including the imposing Entertainment Centre, provided a spectacular backdrop. Retracing his steps to go to work the next day, he found himself travelling across an overpass and down an escalator onto the foyer of Hung Hom station. He tried to carefully pick his way through the throng of people, but whatever he did, it did not seem to be good enough. Suddenly and unexpectedly people would veer across his path. It seemed to him that they were putting their feet where he was about to walk, mid-step, so to speak. He had to suddenly stop to avoid collision. He sidestepped but then someone walked in from the side and he fell trying ever so politely to avoid them. As he lay on the floor, he looked up and pondered the crowds. It seemed to him that the only way to avoid collision, was to simply not look where you were going, or to veer recklessly in and out. It was only then that people noticed and avoided you. It was, he thought, like some kind of insane case of playing chicken with other pedestrians.

As Nickie expected, he found that the mooting culture he encountered at Kai Tak University's law school was aberrant, like a vine planted in the wrong soil and badly fertilised. It was corrupted in Nickie's eyes and student- driven in the absence of professional coaching. The values were not the values of dedication, and the processes of sufficient and in-depth research, multiple drafts of the written memorials/arguments, and intense and frequent oral practice accompanied by detailed and insightful feedback. These things were all blended at the convenience of the students. They simply would not recognise excellence even if they encountered it and, in his early days, he detected a strong resistance coming from the peer group leaders among the mooters. Somehow, bad experience and poor standards and achievement, were mystically elevated in the eyes of the cohort.

His first team to go into battle exemplified the power tussle he had with his students, as he strived to lay down the values, work ethic and commitment required to achieve international mooting success. His Jessup team competed in a Hong Kong round for the right to compete in Washington in the world round of the moot.

The High Court of Hong Kong is located in Queensway on Hong Kong island. He remembered snippets of the action which seemed somehow to capture its essence.

A mooter from the opposing team stood at the lectern, before a panel of three judges simulating the operation of the International Court of Justice.

"Your Excellency, this is justifiable as it represents local customary law."

"Yes, yes, very good," spoke the Chinese judge serving as president of the court.

Nickie rolled his eyes, and whispered ironically to Ramesh who, newly installed as director of mooting, was sitting next to him.

"There really is such thing for the big picture concepts?"

Ramesh said nothing in reply, but wriggled uncomfortably. His thoughts were beyond Nickie's comprehension.

Nickie remembered the awards luncheon. He thought his team had narrowly won each moot he watched. But this was the Hong Kong round of the Jessup Moot, and he did not yet understand that expectation played a governing role, along with the old school tie, in a manner of speaking. At the awards lunch, where the announcement of the winners was made, Nickie sat with his team and Ramesh, feeling gutted by the relegation of his team to third place out of three teams competing. So much effort had been made, so much progress, only to feel the sting of failure in the eyes of the world. He had dragged the team up in performance sufficient enough to succeed but they were still deprived of the winning experience. He knew he had to somehow find a way to give them assurance and support. He did his best to express his pride in the standard they reached but, he knew, at the same time, that their sense of fairness was offended because they had learnt enough to recognise the quality of their performance, that it was better than that of the opposition. Notwithstanding his efforts, he found himself sitting on the MTR as the train flew down the tunnel under Victoria Harbour feeling empty, gutted and saddened about the loss, and feeling he had walked into an ambush. He realised his own naivety, in not realising that there was a barrier for the upstart law school, perhaps only based upon expectation. But it was tangible still, an iron barrier to be blown apart, but he lacked the means to blow it apart for the time being. The status quo prevailed.

The Vis East Moot, a trade law mooting competition that was staged in Hong Kong and in which Nickie also coached provided more opportunities for success. Despite clear progress and a very competent team, the tight and contested nature of the competition meant that a single perverse decision by just one tribunal member could potentially make the difference between merely competing and making the cut for the knockout rounds of the competition. Traditionally, most moots consist of a round robin competition followed by a knockout round.

Nickie remembered the key moment, the moment on which the fortunes of his team turned.

As in all arbitration competitions the mooters from both teams were in a seated position. They wore tags indicating their names and they were mooting to three tribunal members; here, one male and two women. One of the women was an older American woman, from one of the US southern states. It bothered Nickie that she frowned as the HK team mooted, and she also seemed disinterested and impatient, as though she was obliged to hear them but did not enjoy it for a moment. Nickie wondered if she was racist when she seemed to be so entranced by the blonde-haired male mooter from the Danish team.

"To summarise, Mr Chairman, members of the tribunal," said the mooter, "we have argued that the claimant was entitled to avoid the contract, all of the contract, because the non-conforming cars amounted to a fundamental breach and the respondent's offer caused unreasonable interference to my client. I have also argued that the Nachfrist, in accordance with Article 47, subsection 1 of the CISG, was not fixed. And, and (very slow delivery) we also say that 'the Claimant can avoid the contract completely according to Articles 49 and 73(2).'"

At this point the timekeeper held up the TIME card and, prompted by it, the Danish speaker acknowledged:

"Mr Chairman, members of the Tribunal, I see that my time has expired."

The mature Georgian lady, who was not even the chair of the panel intervened, much to the stunned surprise of the other two tribunal members.

"Oh, don't worry about that. I really liked your arguments on the Nachfrist. You make them so well.

Could you go over those again for me? You can have all the time you need."

"Oh, thank you very much madam panellist," responded the handsome Dane, "you make such good points."

It was now shameless in Nickie's eyes. Nickie thought she smiled at the mooter in a sickly, slightly sexual manner. The Kai Tak mooters, Charmaine and Henry, looked at each other with genuine concern. The moot was out of control as the mature American woman's attention hung on every word spoken as if, thought Nickie, she had met again her long-lost childhood love.

By the time the mooter had finished, and the mature Georgian lady had finished with him, another four or five minutes had elapsed. Nickie knew that his team had lost her vote. The best they could hope for was a 2-1 split on the tribunal. However, in this moot it was only the combined raw scores that counted, and, if the mature American lady had, driven by what Nickie took to be her racist nature, marked down the Kai Tak team, that might just be a body blow to their chances of progressing to the knockout rounds. They were soon to learn their fate.

Nickie dreaded the announcement of teams to go through to the knockout rounds. He knew he had to control himself and provide consolation to his team if the worst eventuated and they did not progress to those knockout rounds.

The lecture theatre was crammed with members and coaches of the sixty-four teams competing in the competition. A middle-aged American woman, tall and slim, announced the teams to go through to the knockout rounds of the moot.

"Only three spots left. Team 14 is the University of Washington. Team 15 is the University of Copenhagen."

She paused, and so did the breathing of the members and coaches of forty-eight unaccounted teams in the venue.

"And now to the last spot in the knockouts. It goes to team number 16, the University of Freiburg."

The corridors of the main teaching hall of Kai Tak University were strangely silent that day. Nickie walked along the corridor to find his team in an enclave. Two of the members of the team, both male, were crying. One was very upset, his sobbing was out of control. The other had shed just a few tears and was regaining composure. All members looked gloomy and were perplexed. They were looking at each other with a "what did we do wrong" look. Nickie approached them.

"I know the other Hong Kong teams went through and we didn't. Is that fair, just and reasonable? Definitely not, but I am biased. I want you to know this. You gave me everything. I am proud of your efforts. I know what excellence is. You have achieved excellence and that is how I judge you. The best team does not always win. It's rotten I know, but you need to celebrate your excellence. Well done. You know you have performed brilliantly. Trust your own judgement. Let's celebrate."

Gloom prevailed, but he had tried.

The last of the first bracket of teams Nickie coached for Kai Tak University was for the International Space Law Moot, Asia-Pacific Zone, held in Sydney. Against all expectation back at Kai Tak University's law school, Nickie's team made the final. It was held in the New South Wales Supreme Court between the National Law Academy, Bangalore and Kai Tak University.

The moot seemed close to Nickie until this moment, the decisive moment centring on a detached question of dubious relevance, but that is mooting.

The judge, who was an Australian of middle-eastern descent, good looking and conceited, leaned towards the Kai Tak mooter.

"Agent, this right of innocent passage through air space and into outer space, where does it come from, air law or maritime law?"

The female mooter from Kai Tak University leaned forward as she listened and then rocked backwards for a moment weighing up her options, a choice of two, either air law or maritime law.

"Er... air law."

The judge who had asked the question closed his folder and looked across to the president of the court.

"That wraps up proceedings today," said the president of the court. "We will make our deliberations and see you this evening for the result."

They sat in a coffee shop in the historic Queen Victoria Building in George Street, Sydney. The team and Nickie were ensconced there, tired and relieved that it was at last all over or nearly all over.

The mooter who answered the air law/maritime law question turned to Nickie,

"Dr Jones, how do you really think we went? Did we win?"

"Hard to say," said Nickie. "We didn't have the judge who asked the final question. The answer, to the innocent rite of passage question, was maritime law. The space era did not arrive until the sixties. The right has been referenced in both bodies of law, but the answer he wanted was maritime law. I think he was asking it to separate the teams even though it was not really at issue in the moot. His question was about depth of research. Sometimes judges ask such questions when they have already made up their minds, and are just looking for an excuse to hang their decision on. So, I still hope, but don't necessarily expect, the result to go our way."

"Oh." She was clearly not amused and Nickie realised her loyalty did not run very deep.

That night walking to the awards ceremony, Nickie felt for a moment like a celebrity. He had told the female members of the team to wear traditional Chinese dresses and they had obliged. They were dressed stunningly in their traditional dresses and, as they walked down George Street, Sydney, they looked like movie stars. Pedestrians turned their heads to gape at them.

The venue of the awards ceremony and dinner was a restaurant in the Rocks area at the bottom of George Street, in Sydney's CBD, near Circular Quay and not far from the Sydney Harbour Bridge and the Opera House, Sydney's most recognisable landmarks.

Drinks started before the formal dinner. Bryan, the male member of the team, began circulating among the other teams armed with a glass of Australian red wine, potentially a lethal thing to do if you are small in stature and weight and unaware of the potency of the wine. So easy to lose sight of how much one has drunk. Bryan rose his glass again and again to members of the other teams. He began to lose track of exactly how much he was consuming and how profoundly it would affect someone who was not normally a consumer of alcohol. Consequences followed as he found himself in the male toilet throwing up and dry retching into the toilet bowl.

Nickie was unaware until one of the other mooters, one of the two Floras in the team, drew the situation to his attention.

"Dr Jones, Bryan is still in the toilet."

"Er, okay, I'll have a look."

Inside the washroom, Nickie stood in the general area outside one of the cubicles. He called out, "Bryan,

Bryan, are you okay? Do you think you can come out now?"

"Ahr... soon, soo... Doctor N. Just a few minutes," Bryan replied, half groaning.

"Join us at the table when you are ready," said Nickie. He returned to the restaurant. As he sat at the table, they all looked up as if to say, "Well, where is he?"

"He'll be along shortly," said Nickie to placate the angst. But it soon became evident that Bryan was not quite right.

The dessert was the highlight of the meal. Nickie was taking his first bite when Flora Lee approached him again, and spoke with just a note of reproach in her voice.

"Doctor, Bryan is still in the toilet."

Nickie thought for a short moment before replying "Here we go again." He rose and set off for the rest room.

Nickie managed with patience to coax Bryan out of the toilet. He had thrown up everything that there was to throw up. Consonant with his duty of care to his students, Nickie accompanied Bryan to a nearby taxi rank and they headed back to their base camp, the 'middle of the road' hotel at which they were staying.

Every team that Nickie coached had its special attributes, and carried his love and respect for its student members, all with one exception, a team he christened the team of the two princesses. Not even now would he want to share the trauma of coaching two people who throughout the process thought that they knew more and much better than their coach. Some things are just too painful to even speak about, let alone to write about.

So almost every team was his favourite team. One of his most favoured teams was his 2012 team of Katy, Victor and Larry. Victor had grown up in Singapore and had the habit of elongating certain words, as the Singaporeans sometimes do. Katy spoke Japanese and sang in a pop group, but outwardly, in a law school setting, presented herself as a conventional, strait-laced student. Larry was a true scholar. He had one great attribute for a mooter. He had no fear, and with his brains, he was ideally placed to out-think and out-work even the most perverse or aggressive bench. He also came with a Hong Kong specific mooting disability, namely, that he had been taught English in Hong Kong, Hong Kong style. The Hong Kong English he spoke had certain limitations in terms of the pronunciation of certain words and certain consonants. Larry was one of many who featured in the try-outs for the team.

Chapter 15
The Try-outs for the Last Team

This was Nickie's last team ever. He didn't know it at the time, but a sense of sadness descended upon him, a feeling that everything was about to unravel. He didn't know why he had this feeling. He was empathetic, but he did not see himself as an empath or a clairvoyant. Nevertheless, the feeling clung to him and he had to immerse himself in his deep well of enthusiasm for his job to purge it from the moments associated with beginning this campaign, the first moment being, the choice of a team. The talent, sometimes overwhelming to him, on this occasion was a little on the thin side. But it mattered naught, as long as he secured three individuals to undertake the moot, to commit to the moot, to embrace its values and to pursue excellence during the hard moments, the hard times, to do the hard yards.

Nickie used the Moot Court Room for the try-outs. The mooters blurred before him, although he remembered that Larry kicked off proceedings.

"Your Excellency, I represent the Republic of Granola," said Larry.

"Where?" asked Nickie, "you said the Republic of Granola."

"The applicant state," responded Larry quizzically.

"Oh, you mean *Verona*?" said Nickie with raised eyebrow, gently nudging Larry in the direction of the correct pronunciation.

"Yes," said Larry, "Ranola."

"Oh." Nickie was befuddled and surprised at the depth of mispronunciation he was encountering.

Nickie was soon to discover that the mispronunciation was not restricted to Larry alone. It was more of a systemic thing that did not affect day-to-day conversation to any great extent.

The second mooter at the try-outs stood at the lectern. "And this is not allow-ded."

"So what is dead?" said Nickie who was acting as judge.

"No, Your Excellency, allow-ded. It is not allow-ded."

"Oh," said Nickie in what was rapidly becoming his standard response.

The third mooter at the try-outs Nickie remembered for her repetitive chopping action with her hands. Nickie was mesmerised by her hand gesture, and forgot to listen to her words. His eyes fell steadily under the hypnotic spell of her repetitive chopping action.

With the fourth mooter it was the pen, the twirling pen in her right hand. He watched the pen and imagined the mooter twirling the pen behind her back, and throwing it into the air as the leader of a marching band. Nickie gradually blinked his way back to reality.

"Romeo-22 did not work after its collision with the Juno-1," announced the fifth mooter in the try-outs. Nickie, as judge, was eager to ask questions. "But what…" started Nickie. He stopped speaking as the mooter completely ignored him and continued to speak over him.

"This was damage," he said, and…"

Nickie tried again to ask his question. "But what—" again, he was interrupted by the runaway train that was this mooter.

"And… and… so they are not liable for the damage." Nickie's mouth gaped wide. He sighed and put his hand up in a 'stopping the traffic' gesture.

Patiently, as always, he finally straightened the mooter out on what constituted acceptable courtroom etiquette. "When a judge," said Nickie, "wants to speak you have to go silent. No matter where you are in your submissions, you have to dry up, go silent and listen attentively to the judge's question. And then you have to answer it in a polite and ideally helpful manner. If it is a yes or no question, you answer it simply by saying 'yes' or 'no, Your Excellency'. If it is adverse to your side you may need to go back to a positional statement, explain why, briefly, and then to move on to your next argument." He paused for reaction time, before adding in a kindly way, "Now you know."

The next mooter was a sniffer. Occasionally these come along. The behaviour in question is irritating in the extreme to a judge, and difficult for the mooter himself or herself, because its subconscious nature is not easily recognised or rectified.

"Verona is liable," the mooter confidently asserted, "for the collision between Juno-1 and Romeo-22 under Article 3 of the Liability Convention (sniff). This is because it has not supervised its satellite (sniff)."

"Is there a fault element there?" asked Nickie.

"Yes, yes Your Excellency (sniff)."

"What is fault?" pertinently asked Nickie.

"Well, your Excellency, it is like negligence (sniff)."

"Really?" said Nickie, feigning surprise.

"Yes, your Excellency (sniff)."

"Is that so? (sniff)," said Nickie lampooning.

"Yes, your Excellency (sniff)."

"Please proceed (sniff)." A broad smile appeared on Nickie's face.

The seventh mooter knew his stuff, or so he thought. With the arrogance of youth in the driver's seat, the mooter stood in front of Nickie with firm convictions.

"So," said Nickie, "you are conceding that Verona is liable for its lack of supervision and control over the satellite?"

"No, it is obvious to everyone. Clearly *Montague* is definitely liable. It is impossible for Verona to be liable."

Nickie could not resist feigning sincerity as he responded, but a certain sense of mischief on his part gave him away to anyone who knew about mooting. "Really, obviously, clearly liable, eh?"

"Yes, Your Excellency, obvious."

When it came to declaring who was in the team, Nickie found that those who were selected, had more or less chosen themselves. He assembled the three members in the moot room as soon as practicable. In front of him sat Katy, Larry and Victor. He chose this time to tell them why they were selected. Normally he would not dwell on such things but this time he felt the need to do so.

"Congratulations on your selection in the 2012 Space Law Mooting team for Kai Tak University," said Nickie.

"Thank you," said Katy, and the others nodded their agreement.

"Katy," said Nickie, "you were selected, not because you are a natural talent, but because in the internal mooting competition, you listened and acted on the advice of judges and became better. You have humility and a good spirit, someone I want to work with. And you mooted well at the try-out."

"Larry, you have a few problems with English pronunciation. You tend to pronounce V's as something else. His name is Victor, yes?"

"Yes," said Larry in a kind of sheepish, half-smiling manner."

Rightly or wrongly perceiving the need for further explanation, Nickie blundered forward. "Well, if you pronounced his name like how you pronounce the state of Verona you would pronounce his name Wictor. But it's not that. It's Victor. We can work that out. You also pronounce allowed as allow-ded, something you were taught to do here, but it is wrong, nevertheless. However, your GPA is astronomical. Simply, we need you in order to succeed."

Nickie finally turned his gaze to Victor. "Victor, last but not least. You come across at times as an angry young man, impetuous and impatient. (Victor reacts with a frown) I know you do not think so, but you do have something I value really highly — passion. You speak with conviction and you try hard to persuade. I applaud that. So, you are also an essential part of our team. All three are essential parts of the whole."

Several months later with the written memorials completed and submitted, the team was engaged in their oral training. Katy and Victor were filling the oralist roles for this particular session. The third member of the team, Larry, was sitting quietly. Nickie sat on the bench about to start proceedings. Katy's style when she spoke was a little robotic, but she was reliable and charming and very hard working. Some might not see Katy as a beauty, but she was beautiful with a kind of internal beauty that means that she was entirely beautiful but not in a traditional western, superficial sense.

Nickie opened the practice moot. "This is a proceeding of the International Court of Justice. My name is the Lord Chief Justice on High, Dr Nickie (smiling and laughing at his own puerile attempt at humour), and we have this case concerning on-orbit collision, non-cooperative satellite removal and damages. We have two states here, the Republic of Verona and the Commonwealth of Montague. So can we please have appearances?"

In response Katy moved to the lectern to begin her presentation. "Good morning Your Excellencies. My name is Katy Yeung, appearing on behalf of the Republic of Verona. I will be speaking for fourteen minutes on Montague's liability for damage to Juno 1 under Ground 1 and its liability for the unlawful removal of Juno 1 under Ground 2. My co-agent Mr Larry Ho will submit the issue of space debris under ground 2, and the damage Verona sustained during the monsoonal storm under Ground 3. We seek to reserve two minutes for rebuttal."

Nickie raised his hand in a stop gesture as he turned to Katy's co-agent/co-counsel, Victor.

"Can I ask your co-agent? Is your name Larry Ho?"

Victor smiled as he knew that Katy has been 'busted' for her mistake. "No."

Nickie turned back to Katy, "So who is your co-agent?"

Katy was in process of starting to consciously realise what she has done. Quizzically she offered, "Err Victor Mak?"

"So let's now hear from the applicant state." Nickie nodded approval for Katy to continue.

Gathering herself Katy offered up her case theory:

"Your Excellencies, we are here because the respondent Montague cares more about making money than about fulfilling its international obligations. In preserving its profits Montague caused the loss of Juno 1 and 2, and also the losses suffered by Verona during the monsoonal storm."

She moved swiftly to her roadmap:

"Today the appellant submits on 3 grounds. First Montague is liable for the damage done to Juno 1. Second, Montague is liable for removal of the satellite. Third, the respondent state is also liable for the deaths, terrestrial property loss and environmental poisoning, suffered by Verona during the monsoonal storm. Under the first ground, first, Montague is liable under Article 3 of the Liability Convention. Second, Montague is also liable for failing to give continuous supervision under Article 6 of the Outer Space Treaty. Now moving to the first ground…"

The wall clock seemed to take flight and rolled around in Nickie's mind's eye as quickly as a ball bearing, and Katy concluded, returning to her case theory in doing so.

Katy sat down and Victor rose, moved to the lectern, and waited on the judge to give him the nod to continue.

Nickie always felt that Victor had a mixture of positive and negative elements. There was a slight tendency on his part to come across as an angry young man. This was not something that Victor was consciously aware of, so it seemed beyond his capacity to control. On the other hand, Victor was indeed passionate about what he did, and he had a Singaporean background. He was a local, but his family had lived in Singapore when he was young so that he had the remnants of that amazing Singaporean accent, with its elongated vowels and unique pitch. In this context, in particular, it manifested as a dwelling on the letter 'e' as in Excellency and a tendency to extend the final words in sentences.

At the lectern Victor seemed a little agitated, kind of impatient as he jigged around, instead of exercising composure and control over his body position.

"Good evening, Your Excellency, I am Victor, and I will be making my submission on the debris obligation under Ground 2 and damages under Ground 3. First, Juno 2 is not space debris, and should not be removed. Second, even if Juno 2 is space debris, there is no international customary law obligation to remove space debris."

Although he listened attentively and took notes to provide feedback to the students, Nickie still imagined that the clock was racing forward. Perhaps it was because Victor was so fast, or, then again, perhaps it was because Nickie was so tired.

He tuned in as Victor concluded "…because Verona performed a 'previous internationally wrongful act.' Your Excellency, this concludes submissions for Federal Republic of Montague."

"That is it?" Nickie queried.

"Yes," said Victor suspiciously.

"That's 13-20 not fourteen minutes," said Nickie, "and there is a reason why it is 13-20. Do you know what it is?"

"Err no," responded Victor.

Katy, who had watched Victor attentively throughout his oral arguments, opened up. "It is because he is like AK47."

Katy and Nickie laughed together. "Yes, Katy's got it again," said Nickie. Victor looked slightly incredulous, slightly amused but said nothing.

"I had thought," said Nickie, "that this phrase had nine words in it. "If I could take your excellency to paragraph one." The way Victor says it, it is (he delivered the following as if it was one word in staccato imitation of Victor),

'IfIcouldtakeyourexcellencytoparagraphone',
just one word. After the first minute and a half I wrote down, 'Slow down and relax. Pace is a little too fast.'

You were just going too fast. I liked the passion and intensity of your mooting. You were also nicely waiting for us to go to paragraphs when you used the facts. When you referenced a paragraph, you really waited to dwell on it. You paused. You looked at us. When we were there you continued. That's good. What you need are more pauses. Try to also create some spaces, where you invite the bench to ask you the question you want." As always, Nickie tempered his feedback, by making some positive comments.

Nickie knew that a moot preparation takes seven to nine months if it is done properly and, even then, there is no guarantee that all the hard work will be rewarded. The written memorials have to be prepared so as to meet a deadline, often sometime in February and then there are around six weeks for the oral preparation and then the various regional rounds are conducted, one in Asia-Pacific, one in Africa, one in the Americas, and one in Europe. This time the competition was in Bangalore in India. Somehow the team won their way to the final, which was conducted in the Moot Court Room in the law school there.

The final was between the University of Hyderabad (representing the applicant state) and Kai Tak University (representing the respondent state).

The University of Hyderabad mooter stood and walked to the lectern. It was a large courtroom with a significant audience. The lectern had a microphone, which was really necessary given the size of the room. The audience was seated at the back of the mooters.

The Hyderabad mooter began speaking, but the microphone was not working properly. Within twenty seconds a technician had run to the microphone and fixed the problem. The male mooter for Hyderabad continued to make submissions.

"Your Excellencies, I will demonstrate beyond all doubt that Montague (pronounced 'Mantarg' by this team), is at fault for breaching its international obligation to pay 'due regard to the corresponding interests of other states' as required by Article IX of the Outer Space Treaty. The obligation of due regard requires that Montague balance its interests to take into account the legal rights of other states to pursue their activities on a basis of equality. And this is my point your Excellencies. Montague callously disregarded the rights of other states. Not only have they breached Article IX but also Article III of the Outer Space Treaty. This is because Montague cruelly ignored the risk and did not manoeuvre the Romeo-22 satellite, and this resulted in the collision with Verona's Juno-1 satellite."

Once again Nickie looked up at the wall clock to watch the fourteen minutes of the speaker drift past. His critical faculties were still working, and he could provide feedback to his mooters, but at this stage of the competition, the die had been cast. His job had been done. It was all in the hands of his student mooters, and his job was to let go and to support them if something went wrong.

The Hyderabad mooter concluded. "If I cannot assist your most gracious Excellencies any further, this most humbly concludes my submissions."

Katy walked to the lectern, but had to wait attentively for the Bench to finish their note-taking, and to give her a nod before she could begin her submissions. Eventually the nod came from the president of the court, and Katy began her fifteen minutes of submissions. However, as with the first speaker for her opposition team, she could not initially be heard properly. The microphone was again not working properly. Becoming rapidly aware of the problem at first, she paused, and looked at the technician who studiously ignored her existence. The bench strained its ears. The technician continued to ignore the problem as she continued.

"Good afternoon," said Katy, now barely audible, "Your Excellencies, my name is Katy Yeung, appearing on behalf of the Commonwealth of Montague. I will speak for fifteen minutes on Verona's liability for the damage to Romeo-22 under Ground 1. I will disprove any liability on the part of Montague, for removing Juno-2. My co-agent Mr. Victor Mak, will submit on the issue of space debris and will address the damage suffered in Verona under Ground 3 for thirteen minutes. We seek to reserve two minutes for surrebuttal."

"Your Excellencies, we are here because the appellant Verona argues that Montague is at fault for Verona's own disregard of international obligation. On behalf of the respondent, I argue that Verona's indifference to the safety of other states, has caused the Romeo/Juno collision and the damage of Romeo-22. Further, Verona has no ground to claim for Montague's liability as Verona's indifference to its responsibilities has created grave threats to the satellite systems of the international community with its uncontrolled Juno satellites."

During this time Larry (the third member of the team who was seated in the audience alongside Nickie) and Nickie exchanged looks anxiously. Nickie rolled his eyes and felt nothing but anger and frustration. The audience was also restless because they could not hear the mooter. Nickie whispered through clenched teeth, "Fix the microphone!"

At the six-minute mark the technician sauntered over to the microphone and effortlessly fixed it.

Katy continued, "Additionally, Verona breached its international obligation of continuous supervision and control under Articles VI and VIII of the Outer Space Treaty. Article VIII provides that "a State Party to the Outer Space Treaty, on whose registry an object was entered that had been launched into outer space 'shall retain jurisdiction and control over such object.' And, as already noted, Article VI provides that states are responsible to provide continuous supervision and control over their space objects. Paragraph 7 of the facts tells us that Verona, after failing to restore control over the Juno satellites prior to the collision occurring, made no further attempts to control the satellites. It is Verona who has breached these provisions."

What Nickie had conceived as the decisive moment rolled around on cue. Nickie nurtured hope at the core of his heart. He hoped the team would be listened to and that the ultimate decision would be in their favour, as they had unveiled the lie. They were right to unveil the lie, but things did not work out as he expected.

"Your Excellencies," said the Hyderabad mooter, "a literal interpretation of the term 'caused by' in Article 2 of the Liability Convention only requires a causal connection between the space object and the damage caused. Your Excellencies, the travaux préparatoires clearly indicate that the words were chosen deliberately to avoid the erroneous conclusion that the treaty was restricted only to cases of physical impact."

In short order, Victor found himself on his feet and zeroing in on the lie.

"Your Excellencies," responded Victor, "the agent for the respondent has argued that the travaux préparatoires support an interpretation that the treaty covered more indirect damage than physical impact. They cite the UNCOPUOS meeting of June 1968 in both their orals and their written submissions at footnote 148. (PAUSE) But they do this Court a disservice, because the discussion in the meeting was all about the issue of the protection of nationals of one state residing in another state. It was not as they have said."

When the time came one lie was predictably justified by another lie. There was no retreat based on being shown up. There was an attempt to make out that the speaker had told the truth and the truth-giver was in fact a liar. The principle followed was to win at any cost.

The Hyderabad mooter rebutted. "Your Excellencies, if the agent for the applicant would have looked on the next page of the seventh session reports they would have seen that the discussion was exactly as we stated. The applicant has not made the effort to turn the page."

In the end both rebuttal and surrebuttal were completed and the bench had just a few words to say before it rose. "Thank you," said the judge presiding over the court as president. "This court will now retire to consider its judgement. We will return shortly with a few concluding comments."

The three judges rose as did the audience. They nodded to the audience and then left the room. The audience began to murmur in conversation.

Nickie looked at Larry.

"They lied!" asserted Larry with passion that was untypical for him. "I hope the bench read the minutes of the meeting they referenced."

"Nothing they said about that meeting," said Nickie, "was truthful. But I wouldn't bet my house on it. One lie begets another. We know it's wrong but does the bench care enough to check? We'll see if evil triumphs." He looked shattered and his words left them both feeling shattered, to a lesser or greater extent.

Fifteen minutes later the bench returned to the court. Those in the Moot Court stood. The judges sat and then the audience and mooters followed suit.

The president of the court was a westerner, a somewhat mature man, with a shaven head and a slightly seedy ambience.

"We just wanted to give you a little feedback preliminary to the presentation event, which is in a nearby lecture theatre. We find that the overall standard of all the mooters from both teams was suitably high. There was some argument about the travaux préparatoires. As to the travaux references, well, you know, it all goes to establish the unreliability of the travaux préparatoires in establish the meaning of treaties. Sometimes it is better to look elsewhere." *The Vienna Convention on the Law of Treaties doesn't say that,* thought Nickie.

At that moment Nickie and Larry looked at each other as if to say, "Well that is it — truth is indeed the casualty." There was a sense of loss and sadness in each as they realised that the lies had been at least partially swallowed. Deep down they knew the moot was lost.

When the words finally came, Larry and Nickie were resolute, but Victor and Katy had remained hopeful until the end. The winner of the Asia-Pacific round of the Space Law Moot is... the University of Hyderabad."

The trophies were then presented. For Kai Tak University, a large but bulky trophy that was all sparkles, and instantly started to fall apart, was presented to them as runner-up. Victor, with all his passion, was awarded the trophy as best speaker in the final. And Katy had been sabotaged by the microphone manager so, from Victor's success, she instantly knew she had scored lowest in the final. It was indeed a bittersweet event for her, knowing they had achieved so much and wrongly presuming she was the reason they had lost the final. The photos that they then posed for Nickie to take, so that there would be a record to be publicised back home in Hong Kong, reflected faces that fell short of joy. Their journey would create work opportunities for them, but that was in the future. For the time being they could demonstrate achievement, but not a winning of this competition.

Back at the Margaret River café. the barista peered through Nickie, but he was about to lower a boom gate on him.

"Okay, okay, I've heard enough about your 'kids'. What about you? Why did you leave if you loved it all so much?"

"Politics, cursed politics," responded Nicky, who was already making a deviation from what he knew the barista wanted. "The politics just had to intrude. Promotion, manipulation, it was like an invasion by

Harry Potter's dementors. University politics and ego-driven ambition are like dark, eerie presences; it's like a malevolent mist that hangs around sucking the life out of the souls of idealistic and hard-working scholars. The lying, the obfuscation — these are the tools of trade for those who would take shortcuts to the top of the tree and isn't that almost everyone. Kai Tak University was wonderful but no different to a million other universities with a zillion other self-serving academics.

"Once I was on-board my duties began to grow exponentially. As an idealist I hoped for fairness. As a realist I vaguely sensed they would keep me in my lowly place on the totem pole."

The opening of the Transportation Centre was a major, major event. It was a major initiative of C.K. Yeung, the chairman of the university's council, its peak ruling body apart from the offices of the president of the university and the provost. The president's role was more about policy and key initiatives, while the provost was arguably more like a fixer at the top of the administrative chain, but less of the key decision maker for the university. C.K. was charismatic, diplomatic, a wheeler and dealer with contacts back to the PRC. He had a certain X Factor that would make even the self-obsessed toe the line and fall in behind him. So, for the time being, he was to have his maritime centre. He could now go on television and extol the virtues of the port of Hong Kong, and make reformist noises too with a view to restoring its slipping ranking as a port, then below

Shanghai with its revolutionary island port, and Singapore, a jurisdiction particularly adept at taking others' ideas and making them work better.

C.K. wanted to be seen as a reformer, as someone who could take Hong Kong back to pre-eminence if one day he was to be nominated as Hong Kong's next Chief Executive, the ultimate political prize for an aspiring politician in Hong Kong.

The opening of the Transportation Law Centre, among other things, saw Nickie installed as its Foundation Director. It seemed to him that his name was first in line to do the hard yards to establish problematic and possibly vexed programmes. If he failed it was just another rotten westerner responsible and the hierarchy was untainted. He didn't know if he was fair in seeing it this way, but it was how he felt. The opening of the new centre was held in the multimedia centre of the university and there seemed to be a large number of photographers and some video cameramen present. Nickie recalled the words of Dean Tang, they echoed and re-echoed in his mind because they reflected his position in the state of things within that law school. Ultimately, he was intended, he felt, to be a mere worker, a drone, to achieve other peoples' agendas.

"And Doctor Jones will have to work very, v-e-r-y (elongated for emphasis) hard and it will not be easy. But we will succeed because we aim for excellence and regional pre-eminence. Yes!" Tang finished his speech with a flurry.

Soon, regaled with orchids in their buttonholes, the speakers all lined up to cut the ribbon to mark the opening of the centre.

One of the things that Nickie respected the most about the law school into which he had come was that they celebrated their mooting achievements at a function. This was even so when their mooting programme was embryonic and not successful. He loved the spirit he saw at such times. With success the functions seemed somehow to become politicised, subject to the dean's agendas. One he remembered more vividly than others.

Kai Tak's American provost spoke in his usual manner.

"At Kai Tak University we have a new slogan, 'Adventurers and Discoverers Welcome'. We see mooting as a fine example of this and consistent with our discovery enriched curriculum. Kai Tak University always benchmarks itself against the best in the world. We are among the best in the world, and today we pay tribute to the hard work and dedication of our students."

Dean Tang's agenda dripped from his words. "Professor Shastri has done great work in coaching mooting teams. His teams are the best. He is a very experienced coach."

Ramesh Shastri was invited to speak and, when he did, he too played very liberally with the truth.

"I have coached many teams and they come so close, always so close. Now we are there. We are making finals. Next we will win them."

Then the president of the university and the provost left the event. Only then was Nickie invited to speak by the beautiful female Chinese member of staff who had been chosen to act as master of ceremonies for the event.

Addressing the audience, Nickie was quite brief in his observations.

"All I will say today, is that our mooters have worked long hours researching, analysing, writing, refining, practising and arguing their cases in front of inquisitive and challenging, sometimes perverse benches. It has been a great privilege to be a small part of this process of preparation and to see our students value-added in this way. It has been a privilege and an honour."

Back at Margaret River, momentarily looking the barista squarely in the eyes, Nickie spoke his truth. "I worked extraordinary hours. I was always there. But at the same time, I felt like the invisible man, an exhausted invisible man."

As he spoke, he recalled a particular night of moot training with one of his teams.

Inside the law school video seminar room, the wall clock showed 10.45 p.m. Nickie was finishing off a mooting practice session with his Jessup Moot students.

"Do you want to hear us again?" said Jenny, one of the mooters.

Nickie was muted in mood, very tired, and so he spoke with very slow delivery.

"No," he said, "that's fine. You might not think so, but we are looking good. Every time you practise, you get better. We are nearly there."

When he finally left the room, he shut down the video equipment and the TV screens, turned off the control panel and locked the room. He then walked down empty corridors. As he passed the dean's office he paused in response to a noise and listened for a moment. The noise from inside was that of a man and a woman having sex loudly and about to reach orgasm. *Not again,* he thought, *not here. Please not here too.* One of the voices was that of the dean. Nickie walked back to his room. As he moved off, he shook his head. Back in his room he packed up and left to go home. As he walked along the same corridor, he saw the dean emerging with a pretty young, new female member of staff. When they were just out of hearing, he shook his head and muttered to himself, "Just another alpha male."

Assessment board meetings are part of the life-blood of a law school. Their role is to endorse results and to deal simply with all assessment-related issues including poor performance by students and possible exclusion because of this or show cause notices. There were statistics of results to allow the collective to reflect on grading consistency and so on. Nickie remembered one such meeting that was chaired by the dean of the law school, assisted by the deputy dean of the law school, Tony D'Silva, and serviced by the well-oiled machine that was the administrative staff. Most dominantly representing the administrative side of things was Ellen Sun, assisted by Tina Wong. The administrative support serviced the meeting by providing documents and reports and PowerPoint presentations showing graphs of marks, results, etc.

Nickie remembered one point of business in particular.

"The next item on the agenda," said Tony D'Silva, "is approval for the subject mooting which has been proposed by Ramesh on behalf of the curriculum committee to be a first-year compulsory subject in the LLB programme. Ramesh can you speak to this?"

Ramesh smiled in what Nickie thought was a supercilious, fawning manner as he spoke. "The dean favours including this course in the first-year programme." He paused and looked around exercising his mastery. "Mooting is a priority for the law school and we now, in this subject, have a great opportunity to skill all of our students."

Suri was a serious scholar. He could be stubbornly pedantic, but everyone knew this and most of the staff were attentive and curious about his thoughts.

"Do you really think this is a good idea?" he asked. "Would we be better served by adding a subject on statutory interpretation or a second option in company law? It is a big subject and perhaps we could split it into A and B. What are we really gaining by this that we do not already possess?"

Ramesh responded indignantly. How dare this upstart wish to decline something that he and the dean created in private to be part of an agenda that would see Ramesh promoted to associate professor.

"It teaches skills to everyone. We are a mooting law school. Our reputation and success depend on good training for everyone."

It was at this moment that Nickie chose to speak his mind. He was later to feel that this was the moment when he lost the support of the dean, although that was an elusive matter, because reading the dean was never his forte.

"Surely," said Nickie, "there is a better way, by simply integrating the mooting assessment items as the skills component of key subjects. So for torts, instead of a traditional essay, have them prepare a moot. Look I am a mooting coach. I say we really do not need to overdo the mooting. Integrate the skills and then have internal moots leading on to international mooting. It's a simple formula. It works."

Dean Tang leapt to the defence of his protégé. "Mmm... We say everything for moot. That is our motto. Ramesh can make great success out of this subject."

"Yes," chimed in Ramesh, complacently confident he had the support of the dean, "all for moot. Dean is right."

"This subject is superfluous." Nickie was slowly starting to realise that he was pushing his cart up Mount Kilimanjaro. There was only one way for him and that was down. He thought *I have just leapt from a great height and there is no safety net for me. I'm white and I'm western in an eastern world.*

"Pure folly," muttered Suri under his breath. "Let's take a vote on this," called Suri, exasperated by the futility of even debating a decision, however wrong, that had already been decided behind closed door in the dean's room.

"Yes, thank you Suri," said Tony D'Silva, "That is a very good idea. All those in favour with the creation of a moot subject, please raise your hand." A few hands rose and the collective mood was one of sullenness and resignation. Feigning indifference, he laconically asked, "all those against." Many more hands rose than for the yes vote.

"Thank you everyone."

The meeting thought its will was going to be followed, although perhaps there were some cynics there who knew better. You do not stop the dean.

At a subsequent staff meeting in the multimedia building, the dean rose to address the assembled staff.

"We are good," announced Tang. "We are the best. We want nothing but the best. And I am dean and I want the best. We are simply the best. We aim for excellence when only excellence will do. Mmmm we achieve international excellence and… mmmm… regional pre-eminence. We must go all the way with moot. All for moot. Yes."

Tony D'Silva took the cue, and with a sickly smile he took the microphone.

"We have just one thing to do. That is to confirm the minutes of the previous staff meeting. All those in favour."

Suri, who normally acted with anal calmness, seemed momentarily to lose his calmness.

"Just a moment please. The record of the decision on Ramesh's mooting subject. That's wrong. That is not how I remember it."

"Well this is the record of the meeting," retorted D'Silva showing irritation.

Anita was a young academic from Kashmir in northern India. She seemed to want to prove a point to D'Silva in a fawning kind of way. "The record is correct," she said. "That is what happened. Tony is correct. After discussion, the subject was approved. That's what happened."

"No, not at all. It was not approved." Suri was adamant and there were nods of agreement with this view from around the room. However, it was not as simple as that to achieve an amendment and a return to the original decision. Tony was determined to override the objection, and he rode his bulldozer further into the crowd.

"Well you have heard Anita. Thank you for your response. I take it that it was approved, and these minutes will stand. Now, next item, teaching and learning, the OBTL model."

The eyes within the room universally rolled in response and people look at each other as if they need someone to speak up for the truth and throw himself or herself under the D'Silva tractor. But individually and collectively they were silent, resolute, long-suffering and devoid of the courage to fight on.

Later, in the dean's office, Ramesh Shastri, Tony D'Silva and the dean sat in the dean's comfortable lounge chairs and took tea. The dean's PA had placed the tea set on the table, and began pouring the tea for the three of them. Tang spoke first.

"Is there anything else we can do to assist Ramesh? I want to promote him while I am still dean. Is there anything else you need?"

Ramesh responded deferentially.

"That moot subject will really help. If I can get credit, but you know I have a lot to do as moot director."

"We make it a core subject," said Tony. "If we make it compulsory then Ramesh gets more credit for its introduction."

"Yes," said Tang, "we say moot for everyone. Can we make it a core subject Tony?"

Ramesh had a slight aversion to work. "Do I have to prepare a whole new subject? That will take a long time," he interjected.

"No," said Tang decisively. "Only do enough to get the subject on the books. We make you course convenor, but we get Nickie to teach it. You have credit. He does work for you. Westerners need to earn their money."

Ramesh was fearful again. "But he may object."

D'Silva contemplated the situation and then spoke.

"No. We don't tell him until just before he teaches and there is no time to adjust. He will have to do it. We put him under time pressure. By the time he thinks to complain, it will be too late to change anything."

"Yes," said Tang, "the week before it starts, I will send him an email, tell him you are too busy, badly overloaded, cannot possibly fit it in. He will not challenge if he wants to stay. Have a biscuit," he said, offering chocolate biscuits to Ramesh and Tony.

"You are good," hummed D'Silva with a smile flickering across his face.

"I am the dean. Mmm, that tea makes me feel like eating. Meet me in fifteen minutes outside the Dynasty Restaurant. We have something to celebrate."

The nights were generally very long for Nickie and his students, especially when it approached lodgement deadlines for the written submissions, the memorials that were addressed to the International Court of Justice.

If deadlines were pressing, the students would sometimes have to complete a final all-night session to be able to lodge the written submissions on time. Nickie encouraged completion earlier than the date due, because he knew from hard experience something of the things that can go wrong when students are lazy, vacillate and simply refuse to be timely. On this night, the clock in the corridor near the Law School showed 4.30 a.m. Nickie, looking tired, emerged from the Moot Court and walked down the corridor to his room. Inside he gathered some papers and his backpack. Then he walked along more empty corridors until he came to an elevator that was not running any longer because of the hour. He had to walk down the stairs, and he found himself taking long steps and hoping not to trip and fall. He walked to the front entrance of the university. The security staff nodded and let him out into the pre-dawn.

Outside Nickie could not walk down the tunnel to Celebrity Mall as it was closed. Instead he climbed steps to find that there were no taxis on the road above the underpass. A few old ladies and gentlemen stood in a group as they were starting their tai chi exercises before dawn, before the dragon that was this city, awoke.

At the train station Nickie sat forlornly on a seat, waiting for an early train. He felt spent, as if he had barely enough energy to move. Although he loved Hong Kong and its lifeblood sailed through him like a river, this image, for him, in his memory's minds-eye, captured the feel of all the hard yards and unrecognised, unseen labour he had undertaken for the love of his work and his students.

Back at Margaret River township, he looked directly in the eyes of the barista. Question marks hung in Nickie's eyes as a kind of vagueness descended upon him.

"Perhaps I should tell you about my last campaign in Hong Kong, I mean China. It took us to India."

At that second, Nickie's mind was back in Bangalore in the taxi leaving this vibrant but busy city. He recalled for a moment or two the taxi being chased by wild dogs as it drove along a ramp taking it onto the main freeway in Bangalore. The students and Nickie looked back as the cab out-raced the dogs.

Back at Margaret River the rain kept pouring down. The barista, it seemed, was tiring of Nickie's stories of woe. The barista's words were almost like a stop sign, but not quite.

"I get the picture about academics. Was there nothing else? No, well... *action* if you don't mind me asking?"

"I loved my work, but it was as nothing compared to a certain friendship. Of everything that I saw and experienced in Hong Kong the most important thing for me was Tina, Tina Wong. I first became really aware of her when she revised the law school website. She sent an email with a link to the proposed revision and it was good. Instead of taking her work for granted, I flicked her an email in appreciation. Too many good people in academia are taken for granted, used and not acknowledged. The egos and the agendas dominate."

Chapter 16
Be Still my Beating Heart

Tina worked hard throughout the day on her varied tasks. She typed into her computer, played to perfect the law school website, spoke to colleagues on various matters, answered the telephone and listened politely to her colleagues and boss.

On this day, when Nickie logged into his computer, he went first to emails and there he saw a bulk email from Tina to all the law school academic staff. He studied the email for a period and then he began to type an email response to Tina. It read as follows:

"Dear Tina,

I had a look at the new website and, as you asked for feedback, here goes.

I think it was great, very professional and I like the use of blue for law. Big improvement. Congratulations. Very well done. Good job!

Best Wishes,

Dr Nickie Jones"

Later, in the law school central administration office, Nickie was speaking to Daisy, a long-term member of the law school office staff.

"Thanks, Daisy, for all your hard work on this. It looks like all systems go. The bookings look good."

"Everything is signed," replied Daisy. "All forms are in. Don't forget to keep receipts. We will need them for accounts."

"We will," said Nickie reassuringly.

While he was speaking, Tina had uncharacteristically looked up from her work and noticed his presence. Tina walked out of her room and approached Nickie just after he left Daisy.

Tina initiated contact. "Professor," said Tina affixing her eyes to Nickie's own as she spoke, "thank you so much for your gracious comments about the new law school website. I appreciate your kind words."

Then followed a kind of absent-minded pause and everything seemed to go in slow motion for an instant. Somehow Nickie felt surprised as he had not paid the attention he ought to have towards Tina's role. He fumbled for words, the right words.

"I was only speaking the truth. The site looks great. You have done a wonderful job. Well done."

It was morning in Hong Kong, a grey dawn due to the smog squeezing down from the Pearl River Delta industrial sites. Nickie walked slowly up a ramp at Hung Hom to the freeway and the crossing lights. He crossed the freeway at the lights and walked into the Metropolis Centre and up the escalator into the foyer. From there he walked onto the bridge above the road and into the Hung Hom train station, where he waited for a train. As always in Hong Kong there was never long to wait on the platform. Within a minute or two the train doors opened, and people jostled for any seats available. The people sat in their seats and most people paid attention only to their devices, the phones, and the iPads or equivalents. Above them the television screens in the carriage were active with news stories punctuated by advertisements for toothpaste or cosmetics.

When Nickie entered his office at work he sat at his desk and opened his computer. His first port of call was his email. He opened an email, which read:

"Staff Changes

This is to advise that Ms Tina Wong is leaving the Law School. She is moving to the Office of the Vice-President. For the time being Ms Annie Chung will serve in the role of Assistant Office Manager.

We wish Tina well in her new position.

Ellen Sun

Office Manager"

Later that day Nickie came across Tina in a law school corridor. He found himself walking in one direction, with Tina walking in the opposite direction towards him. Nickie initiated contact.

"I understand you are leaving us for the vice-president's office. Congratulations with your new position. You will be sorely missed. I will miss you, but I know you will succeed."

Tina responded shyly, "Thank you."

They looked at each other momentarily and smiled.

"I'd better go to my meeting," said Tina, "goodbye."

Nickie nodded and walked on. Tina stood in the corridor looking at him walking away. She opened her mouth to say something, but then closed it again, not quite sure exactly what to say.

Three months passed before they met again in Celebrity Mall and then purely by chance.

Nickie was walking on the ground floor around a corner near the Brooks Brothers shop. She was dressed in a cream-coloured dress and somehow looked very beautiful. She was a mature Chinese woman, not a twenty something Chinese woman. But she still had her slim figure and looked as though she was barely thirty years old, although she was much older. She had a certain kind of innocence about her.

Nickie was pleasantly surprised to encounter her in this way.

"Hello," he said.

"Hello," said Tina who was also pleased.

There was a pause as each looked at the other and they both reached out and touched arms. As they did, time stood still for Nickie and everything seemed to move in slow motion. In that instant Nickie saw himself, much older, lying in Tina's arms. Tina's hair was streaked with grey hair. He looked up at her face which still, despite the grey, despite the age, carried her beauty. He was stunned because he felt he was seeing his own dying, a dying that was occurring in Tina's arms. Nickie also saw in a split second an image of the waters of Sai Kung Harbour and the prow of a boat.

In another instant Tina and Nickie withdrew their arms as if there had been a flash of electricity that passed between them.

"Nice to see you," said Nickie.

"Yes, me too," responded Tina.

They were both affected but both shy and could not articulate their feelings. As they parted Nickie was moved to speak.

"Bye," he said lamely.

Tina smiled, nodded and walked on.

Nickie sat in his office at the law school, Kai Tak University. He was pensive, engaged in an internal debate and then he decided. His fingers tapped on the computer keyboard. He typed the following email to Tina:

"Subject: Catching up

Message:

Dear Tina,

It was nice to see you the other day in Celebrity Walk. I wondered if you might like to catch up properly and to have lunch together. If this is inconvenient, I will understand but if we could meet for lunch that would be great.

Best Wishes,

Nickie"

Nickie waited for some time outside the restaurant in Celebrity Mall that Tina had designated as their meeting place. He was slowly learning rule one in his relationship with Tina, that she was always late. He was later to learn her star sign was Aquarius, the sign of procrastination. It was part of her mystique to always keep men waiting.

Nickie waited anxiously, looking at his watch. Tina arrived, walking fast.

"Sorry. Urgent job to do for vice president before I could take lunch."

"The price of promotion," observed Nickie. "Your job is quite significant now. More important than in law school. Yes?"

"Busy anyway," conceded Tina.

In the restaurant they were shown to a table and then sat down. The restaurant, like so many of the western-style restaurants in Hong Kong, such as Dan Ryan's or Amaroni's, was arguably a dominantly western-style restaurant but with the hint of fusion between eastern and western cuisine.

Nickie thanked the waiter as they were given the menus from which to make their choices.

Tina's respite was short-lived as her mobile phone rang yet again…

Speaking in Cantonese Tina responded "Yes, oh, outside practice file in J drive, outside practice file — law school, Conflict of interest part. Yes. That's it. See you."

("無錯, 喔, 校外執業檔案 - 法律學院, 利益衝突既部份。 無錯, 就係咁。 咁遲啲見")

Her attention momentarily diverted, Tina now turned her attention back to Nickie.

"Sorry, work. Better to fix now."

"Busy girl," he said thinking also of the John Hurt character in the movie *Contact* whose words he seemed to be repeating almost involuntarily.

"Yes."

"Are you hungry?" asked Nickie.

"No." After a brief pause "You?"

"Not really," replied Nickie.

Tina smiled and with pleading eyes suggested, "We could share?"

"Great idea," said Nickie relaxing.

When the food came Nickie was about to plunge his fork into some food when Tina bowed her head, crossed herself, and began quietly saying grace prior to eating.

Nickie was pleased that Tina wanted to share. In his mind's eye he reflected back to his wife who generally chose the most expensive item on the menu. Sharing was a novel but joyful way of eating in Nickie's eyes. He felt a beautiful innocence about what was going on between Tina and himself. It was a wonderful way to begin their friendship.

They talked as friends do about everyday things, like people they had worked with in the law school. Tina spoke a little about her family situation. She would never elaborate much, because real openness was always a bridge too far.

"So," said Nickie, "you were married, and you have two children?"

"Yes," replied Tina. "My husband left me. My children were both under ten. It was very hard. He said I focus only on the children and neglect him. Women from mainland China give him more sex. They are more aggressive. I am traditional Chinese. Traditional Chinese women are passive. My husband had many affairs and then he left me. My in-laws all blamed me. They said it was my fault."

Nickie responded and almost immediately felt ashamed of his response. It was typically Australian and blunter than he really was. "You couldn't tell them to 'get stuffed'?"

Tina looked knowingly at him. This man clearly had to be educated about 'things Chinese'.

"No. That is not the Chinese way."

"How old are your children now?" Nickie enquired.

"Nineteen and seventeen. My daughter goes to Cambridge University. My son will go to Oxford."

Vaguely aware of the inevitable sacrifices that Tina would have made, Nickie responded. "Impressive. You and they must have worked hard to achieve this."

"Yes… they have. (pause) I devote my life to my children and my family. I am traditional Chinese."

Nickie's feelings for Tina were always strong, from that first moment when they reached out and their arms touched in Celebrity Mall. He could not understand quite why, other than to think of it in terms of fate having brought them together. He doubted that he could persuade her into his bed, but she was coming to see him in his apartment.

Nickie opened the door. Tina stood there, dressed in silk business attire, a coat and a dress. She wore black shoes, which she discarded in the Asian way when she entered the apartment.

They kissed deeply but then she eventually drew away from him.

"No," said Tina.

"Please," begged Nickie.

He kissed her again. She drew away again.

"No."

"Tina, I love you. Please." He had nowhere else to go if she persisted.

Tina paused and thought and looked at him knowingly. Having considered during the long silence she smiled and with a sparkle in her eyes she spoke.

"Yes."

This was the beginning of so much beautiful lovemaking. Nickie was discreet so he did not convey very much of what actually occurred, other than the beginning of a love affair that lasted for around four years. In his own head he remembered, treasured so much every moment, but he could not open up to anyone about the exquisite feelings and the beauty he felt, the feelings of total love that not even in the early days of his marriage had he experienced. He remembered Tina naked, but always shy about her body.

She was shy too about the size of her breasts, which were small, but what her breasts did not possess in terms of size her beautiful nipples more than made up for. He could not say it to the barista, but Tina was a moaner. This was not much different from many other Asian women but not so prevalent in the west. Because of this Nickie always felt appreciated. He always felt that the lovemaking was being enjoyed on both sides.

And then there was the moment he most enjoyed, he most savoured, a moment the memory of which was emblazoned on his soul forever.

They had made love and were still in bed. Tina's beautiful black hair caressed Nickie's mouth. She fell asleep. He was awake, soaking in her beauty and his own joy in having made love to a woman of internal as well as external beauty. He could feel some of her hair between his lips. She breathed easily as she slept. He felt in that moment a sense of total trust, total intimacy. The great love he felt, a love that comes to few people to experience in this lifetime. He felt the joy of love, the great privilege of love, the truth of love, the purity of love: a moment so exquisitely beautiful that it would last him all the days of his life. He hoped for many more, but life is cruel and what we prize so much can sometimes be taken away from us, withdrawn from us so unjustly, inexplicably, irrevocably.

He never forgot Sai Kung. Sai Kung was a fishing village in the New Territories. It had an exquisite and sweeping harbour that was littered with islands, a frequent backdrop for locally made movies. The shorefront had a wide walking space that separated a long line of seafood restaurants from the boats that were moored to the shore. One could walk out along the pier to survey more boats sporting their most recent catches. In the restaurants along the shore, the fish were kept alive swimming around in glass aquariums. You could choose your own fish and consume it after it had been cooked, the freshest seafood possible in this life.

On this occasion a street or two away from the waterfront a few cattle had wandered onto the roads. The locals treated them with respect and worked around them for the time being.

As Tina's car approached Sai Kung, she spoke. "Thank you for the CD. I often listen to music when I drive, especially when I play tennis on Saturday mornings with my friends."

"You like driving?" Nickie asked.

"I love driving. But I drive slowly. My son says I drive too slowly. He thinks I should drive faster."

Tina drove her car up a ramp onto a roof top, semi-empty car park. Despite the beautiful locale, the day was a typical bleak, wintery day. Inside the car, Nickie and Tina looked at each other in silence. In unison they leant across and kissed in long lingering kisses. Eventually they stopped and looked at each other tenderly. Nickie caressed Tina's cheek with his hand.

Nickie and Tina walked towards the restaurant strip, the fish restaurants at Sai Kung. They stopped and posed for photos (Nickie carried a camera), near a V-shaped corner of the waterfront with long boats of differing colours including red, green and light blue moored there in the background. Behind these, four or five islands were visible in the harbour. Nickie produced the camera and took a photograph of Tina and Tina in turn reciprocated.

At the waterfront on a pier Tina spoke to an old lady in a boat and negotiated a fee for hiring the boat and her services to take them around the harbour.

In Cantonese Tina asked, "One hundred and fifty?"

"One hundred and seventy-five," said the old lady. "That is the best I can do."

Tina nodded to the old lady and turned to Nickie. "Pay her one hundred and seventy-five dollars."

Tina and Nickie boarded the boat. They sat close beside each other, on a low bench at the side of the boat as it slowly left the wharf and dawdled out into the harbour.

Nickie took photos of the harbour and of Tina. Tina posed on the prow of the boat kneeling, and he was really enjoying being out on the water and the motion of the boat and her company. Although it was a coolish, overcast day the water was calm and beautiful in its grey/green colour. Tina wore a light blue felt top and Nickie wore a dark blue jumper and the cap of his favourite Australian football league team, the Saints (St. Kilda).

Nickie handed the camera to Tina and made his way to the prow of the boat and knelt for a photograph, however, his balance was not as good as Tina's balance and he fell, but thankfully not out of the boat. Seated unceremoniously he looked up at Tina and they both smiled and laughed. The old lady also joined in and had a quiet laugh.

Nickie dipped his hand down into the water and lifted it up to touch his face and then Tina's face like he was performing some ancient ceremony. They held hands. He looked into her sparkling eyes and she into his eyes.

"It is so beautiful," said Nickie stating the truth that both saw and felt.

As they walked among the shops at Sai Kung they discussed where to have a coffee. Tina strode ahead and pointed to a particular coffee shop/bakery. She was uncharacteristically excited.

"They make special cakes here," she says. "You know Portuguese tarts. My favourites."

Nickie took off his St Kilda football club cap and placed it in front of him on the table at which he was sitting while Tina placed the order at the counter.

A Chinese man sitting with family at the next table smiled on seeing Nickie's cap and spoke to Nickie.

"My team too. We lived in Melbourne. That was our team. Good team."

"I supported them since I was three years old," said Nickie, "but we have only ever won one premiership.

This doesn't matter because this team is our tribe. We are from the same tribe!"

When Tina sat down, she seemed very animated, somehow very alive, less reserved than her usual demeanour. She seemed optimistically interested in everything. "They will call me when it is ready," she said.

Nickie could not restrain himself. "You have always seemed so very shy. Now you seem so very happy."

"At work I focus on what I have to do," said Tina. "I give it all my attention, but it is not me. When work is over each day, I am alive. Yes, I am shy, but not so much with my friends. With my close friends I am open. Normally I am not an open person."

Nickie remembered all the beautiful moments that followed this day. Rightly or wrongly he felt it was the highlight of his life, a day of complete and unrestrained happiness and joy. But there were other days that were special to him too; indeed, every moment with Tina was a moment of joy and delight. He remembered seeing her off into a minibus at Hung Hom and watching her sitting in the bus as it moved off. He recalled their time at the zoo, on a half-empty train with an old Chinese woman sitting opposite looking at them, knowing there was a special relationship, sensing the love. And there was the time they walked along the waterside at Hung Hom in the direction of Kai Tak with the exquisite Victoria Harbour bordering their love.

He also remembered the lovemaking between the two of them, although it was not seemly to speak about it to others. Every moment seemed like an eternity dipped in the love of the gods. Nickie never knew such happiness was possible in this lifetime. But just as his joy seemed so deep, suddenly everything changed, suddenly, unexpectedly his tower crumbled. Its bricks turned to sand and his life was changed again, but 'why' he did not know.

After the dean had turned against him and indicated his contract would not be renewed, Nickie was left with no other viable employment alternative in Hong Kong. He had no choice but to seek a position in Australia and to return there for work. He had hoped to persuade Tina to join him and, at first, Tina was making all the right noises. She asked eagerly about life in Australia. Was it as safe on the streets as Hong Kong? What about the tax system? Was it based on a flat tax like in Hong Kong? What about real estate?

Nickie always had hope in his heart. He took it for granted that he and Tina would get together, become man and wife and relocate to Australia. He knew she had a family and that she was devoted to all her family, but it had never stopped them before. He was confident, full of joy as he approached their meeting in the Celebrity Mall.

Tina and Nickie sat together in silence. She looked as she normally did, as if she was transacting business, but was not personally engaged. She looked as if she was involved in doing a mundane task, nothing out of the ordinary (or at least this was how Nickie thought about it later). Nickie, on the other hand, looked shocked, mesmerised, dumbfounded and searching for words to ask the questions he desperately needed to ask. He felt like his heart had just been ripped out of his chest.

"What happened?" asked Nickie.

"Can't say," shrugged Tina.

"But" pleaded Nickie, "you have to tell me something."

"I feel conflicted."

"What do you mean? How? Why?"

"I am traditional Chinese," pronounced Tina.

Nickie protested. "That should not stop us. Different races, different traditions. It all means nothing."

"I cannot express my emotion," said Tina. "I am conflicted."

For a moment, a wall of silence descended between them which Tina eventually broke.

"You cannot understand. You are not Chinese. It is against my religion to have sex outside of marriage. We cannot have sex any longer."

"But what..." asked Nickie the drowning man, "what if I ask you to marry me?"

Tina had all the answers as if she had rehearsed everything in her mind and it was going to plan. There had to be nowhere for Nickie to go, no plea to which he could have access.

"Then I have to ask my children. It is not fair to them that I have sex outside of marriage. I dedicate my life now to my children and my family. I have promised them. I do not want anything for myself."

The door was indeed being closed upon Nickie, and he felt both the shock of loss, and the defeat of his mind for he had no pleas, no smooth words, no emotional appeals that he was capable of making. His heart had just been shredded and he had allowed it to happen with barely a whimper. Mostly he felt shock.

"But…" Nickie's words had all but disappeared now as Tina began to ready herself to depart.

"I have to go," said Tina, "sometimes things do not last. They have their time and that is it. They are gone. We are still friends but… I do not love you."

Nickie tried to dig inside himself to say something but only the beginnings of another "But" issued forth and then Tina was gone, leaving quickly, clinically.

Nickie sat in his office for a very long time looking at the computer screen. He had never trawled the Facebook pages of others. However, he was so mesmerised by the curtain that Tina had drawn down on their lives together that he felt the need to search anywhere for an answer. He felt she had not told the truth. 'Yes,' she was a devout Christian and 'yes' she was dedicated to her family, her broader family outside her children.

Nickie found himself trawling through the Facebook pages of Tina's friends. He opened the Facebook page of one of her Facebook friends and found a photo there of Tina at a table with others in a restaurant at night. She was sitting next to a Chinese man who was her date. All of the people at the table were toasting with glasses of Australian red wine. Tina and the man sitting next to her were smiling; their shoulders touched as they leaned against each other and she had a look of happiness on her face, joy in the moment.

The day ended and a long sleepless night for Nickie gave way to the dawn of a new day in Hong Kong.

Nickie sat in a chair in his apartment gazing at the desktop computer screen in front of him.

Email from Nickie:

"*Subject: Respect and Understanding.*

I feel you have hidden your choices behind the shield of religion and family without being honest with me while perhaps hoping I would go away without ever having to tell me the truth. Please tell me the truth.

Love,

Nickie"

Email reply from Tina:

"*Subject: Re Respect and Understanding*

Dear Nickie,

Thank you for your frank sharing. I will respond later.

May God bless you every day.

Love,
Tina"

The rain in Margaret River township was abating at last. The storm had left a sky full of grey clouds in its wake, with just a few flurries of rain every now and again. It was as if the sky was soon going to clear and there would be a return to those beautiful, endless Australian blue skies. In the Margaret River township coffee shop, Nickie looked at the barista squarely in the face.

"She never did get back to me."

"Not ever at all?" asked the barista who was used to plain-speaking country girls who never kept a secret all their lives long.

"Never," said Nickie, "not to this day. So you see, there is just me and Spider. My dog gives unconditional love, don't you Spider; but my dog is not traditional Chinese."

"Sixty ways to leave your lover. You don't have anyone here?"

"When I was in the East," said Nickie, "I was struck by lightning and that was it. I wanted the lightning to strike twice but somehow the rules of the cosmos do not allow for that. That was it for me for this life. There was only one person, one love for all time or no love for all time. I became a one-woman man. Just room enough in the heart for one big love or no big love at all."

The rain had stopped fully, and the sun's rays were poking through the cloud cover. The beginnings of a beautiful rainbow began to appear in the sky.

Nickie looked at the dog but spoke also to the barista.

"Time to go Spider. Thank you for your hospitality. I appreciate it."

Nickie and the dog walk from the coffee shop and onto the footpath. The dog shook itself as dogs do around water. They started the walk home. But then Nickie paused, knelt next to the dog and patted it on the head.

"You know Spider, when I walked with her, I walked in heaven. No one could ever compare. I really loved her Spider."

Nickie straightened himself a little stiffly and resumed the walk home. Nickie looked down at Spider and the dog looked up with big eyes wide open to communicate. Spider's tongue licked its chops in anticipation of the evening's meal.

"I know. You want some tucker. It won't be long now." He paused to contemplate, and his mind went back to those days in Hong Kong and the sadness that became part of his life.

Nickie spoke to Spider out loud.

"You know, I never knew. I never knew why she went off me. I never knew if it was really someone else, or her dedication to her children, or just wanting to live a purely selfish life to nurture her ego by gaining attention. I don't know. My life is a question mark, Spider."

They walked along a little further. Nickie looked up at the sky. The rainbow held firmly in the sky. The sky was spectacular then in the late afternoon, a double rainbow, that rarest of things in nature.

As he looked up at the awesome rainbow, he remembered again the most tender moment in his life when Tina lay beside him in the bed in his apartment in Hong Kong those years before. She was asleep. Some of the hair from her head lay across his mouth. He had framed this memory in the landscape of his mind's eye. He felt it would stay with him forever. He remembered it again and again, like the video of a favourite movie.

Nickie continued his discourse with his beautiful dog.

"You know Spider. I never stopped loving her. Not for a second. Not for a minute. All my life. For all eternity."

They walked further. Nickie's legs stumbled to a stop.

Nickie and his dog were right alongside a church. He entered the church with his dog. He held his hand to his heart and reached out with his other hand to pat his dog which sat in the aisle, attentive and concerned.

"Broken heart," Nickie muttered to himself.

He remembered sitting in a coffee shop at Kai Tak University with Tina.

"Can we go back to my room? Will you let me hold you in my arms to say goodbye, even if we cannot make love?"

"No," replied Tina. "I live here, and everyone knows me. People will see. I do not want to have a bad reputation."

He also remembered leaving after another failed journey to Hong Kong, another failed attempt to reconcile.

Nickie and Tina were standing just at the door to the taxi rank at Celebrity Mall. After Nickie placed his bag in the boot of the taxi, he turned to Tina. They shook hands. He held her hand for a second longer.

"Can you give me a hug?"

"Traditional Chinese women do not show emotion in public."

"Oh," murmured Nickie.

"Goodbye."

"Goodbye," echoed Tina with a flippantly optimistic energy.

Nickie rode away in the taxi for the last time.

Returning from his memories of the past to the present moment in the church, Nickie leant down and patted his dog. He felt unwell and was sweating. His breath became shallow but more rapid and his heart was racing.

"I always thought we would make it, come back together again. Never did. She stole my heart and soul Spider. Stole it and never gave it back properly."

Nickie reached into his jacket and took out a locket. He opened it to reveal a small photo of Tina in it. A single tear rolled down his cheek.

"Still does it. Still brings a tear to my eyes, Spider."

Nickie's body went limp as it lurched forward in the pew and the locket fell from his hand. The chain attached to the locket was around his hand and the image of Tina hung in mid-air suspended from his hand. Spider rose to his feet, whimpered and tried to lick Nickie's face.

The cloud above the steeple of the church momentarily moved across the sun and rain again began to pelt down.

Epilogue

Tina was having dinner with her family in her villa apartment. Her son and daughter sat at the table with her father and one of her brothers and there sat also her seven-year-old daughter. The daughter has Eurasian looks. They were all happily eating and speaking in Cantonese. Then there was a knock on the door answered by her Filipino maid. She came to Tina and whispered in her ear.

Speaking in Cantonese Tina excused herself. "Please excuse me. I must go to the door."

A mature European man with a serious look on his face stood on the steps to her apartment.

The man spoke to her and then her head dropped, and she looked at the ground with a sense of shame and sadness. Tina, in sombre mood, then looked at the man squarely in the eyes.

"Thank you very much. It is not easy."

"One last thing," said the man, "he wanted you to have this". The man handed Tina a locket, Nickie's locket which Tina scrutinised. She nodded and the man left. She waited a moment to compose herself.

She walked back inside to the table with background talk in Cantonese going on around her. She sat there silently looking down at her plate. She was trying hard to close off all emotion.

Tina's father, speaking in Cantonese, asked, "What is wrong precious flower?" She slowly raised her head, looking at him first and then with a tear running down her cheek, and looking now at her seven-year-old daughter, she spoke in a very measured way.

"Her father is dead."

She bowed her head in prayer then excused herself from the table.

A boat steered by an old lady slowly ploughed its way on a rainy day across the expanse of the harbour at Sai Kung, outwards until Tina, who was sitting in the boat along with her seven-year-old daughter, spoke quietly, respectfully to the old lady in Cantonese.

"Stop here, this is a good place. Thank you."

Speaking to her daughter Tina said, "Be quiet now. Mummy has to pray and say goodbye to someone special."

"Yes Mummy," said her daughter in English, looking up with eyes wide open. Tina bent down with a small box and lifted its lid.

"Betty, help Mummy to empty this container."

Together they held the box out over the water and Tina reached over to open the lid, and then its powdery contents emptied into the wind, some settling momentarily on the surface of the water. Tina then replaced the box into a dark shopping bag she had with her and took two flowers out of it.

"One for you. One for me. Here throw it out into the water like this. It will float."

The daughter smiled innocently, lovingly, at her mother and threw the flower onto the surface of the water. It floated. The boat engine started up and the boat turned back towards the shore. The two flowers remained floating on the waters of the harbour.

The car park was the same one that Nickie and Tina once parked in. Once again there are few cars parked there on this rainy week day.

Tina and her daughter got into her car. Once inside they buckled up. Tina helped her daughter Betty with her seatbelt, thoroughly checking it like a good Hong Kong mother would. Then she turned to drive off but is frozen. A tear comes to her eyes and she looks up at the sky. Her face is now a sea of tears.

"I am so sorry."

She then took Nickie's small gold locket from her bag and hung it from the front mirror of the car.

"Mommy, what's wrong?" asked her daughter.

"I made a mistake. Have you ever made a mistake darling Betty?"

Betty answered uncertainly, probing for approval and hoping she was not in trouble.

"No?"

She smiled the disarming smile of a beautiful child of that age.

Tina smiled in return through the tears.

"I am sorry Nickie."

A single car drives from the car park and looks insignificant from the distance in a city of many millions of souls.

"Mummy, who is Nickie?"

"Nickie was your father. I am sorry you never knew him, but I tell you his name now. It is my gift to you."

"Mummy, I like Sai Kung. Can we come here again?"

"Yes darling. All our lives we will come back here. I'll stop the car. Give Mummy a hug."

As Betty embraces her mother tears stream down the mother's face.

A single ray of light, of joy, of hope shines through a gap in the clouds.

The End

www.ingramcontent.com/pod-product-compliance
Lightning Source LLC
La Vergne TN
LVHW091537060526
838200LV00036B/651